I0768694

A DESIRE TO BE FREE

A COMING-OF-AGE NOVEL

A DESIRE (VOL. I)

IVORY RAVEN

LJ MARSHALL'S
PUBLISHING HOUSE

Copyright © 2019, 2024 by Ivory Raven

All rights reserved.
No part of this publication may be reproduced, stored, or transmitted in any form or by any means, electronic, mechanical, photocopying, recording, or otherwise, without the prior written permission of the Publisher.

ISBN: 979-8-9914097-3-5

ISBN: 979-8-9914097-1-1 (e-book)

Published by LJ Marshall's Publishing House
An imprint of Aoshiki Press

Names, characters, places and events are products of the author's imagination, and any resemblances to actual events or places or persons, living or dead, is entirely coincidental.

CONTENTS

MICHAEL

ANOTHER PEACEFUL EVENING AT BRIERLEY GEN AVENUE. Michael hopped out of the limousine and walked into his so-called palace. He was welcomed by a butler who held the door open. "Evening, sir. How was the ceremony?" inquired the butler as Michael handed him his suit jacket.

"Why don't you ask my father? He was the one who got invited; I was merely an unwelcomed guest," he walked past the butler and towards his room.

Michael had a pleasant life up till now. His father, Larry Walker, was a judge who made a comfortable living and was now nominated as Los Angeles's district attorney. Michael's mother, Lisa Walker, is currently a psychiatrist, who also makes a comfortable living. Therefore, this afforded Michael the opportunity to live a luxurious life. He lives in a palace-like villa with butlers and security guards. Michael lived there since his birth. His parents gave him everything he could dream of, limousines to and from school. Plus, Michael had the best education in the region. Basically, he lived a life anyone would want to live. But it came at a cost, him, the eldest son.

Michael's life was so strict that he had no social life. Butlers were following him everywhere in the house, and he had no friends at all. His sister, Isabella, was treated as a queen. She was five years younger than Michael and was dominating the whole family. Her word was absolute. Michael was surprised that his mother, who is a psychiatrist, couldn't notice they are not treating their children equally. While his sister gets to enjoy her life, Michael had to deal with dressing formally and going to ceremonies with his father. According to his parents, Michael is the family's face. They wanted him to be perfect—flawless. Well, that doesn't bother him as much as the fact that he can't make any decisions on his own. Michael wanted to be an architect while his father wanted him to be a judge. Michael just wants to live his life the way he desires, and to have a social life. But his parents had other plans for him.

It's the last week of the finals, and Michael was on edge. The fact that they locked him in his room just makes him crazy. He could go to the bathroom three times a day, and his food was delivered to his room. Other than that, Michael was sealed inside his room with nothing but his bed, studying desk, and a small library for references. He used to have an entertainment room with all his stuff. But it was locked since the beginning of the finals. It's not that Michael has terrible grades; in fact, he has been the top student for the past three years. But his parents always said it's normal for the son of a district attorney to be the first. They never praised him, not even a 'Good job, son'.

The next morning, Michael had his calculus final exam. It

was a piece of cake, for him at least. While exiting the class, Michael turned around and faced the class. He was laughing deep inside, seeing all those students struggling with the exam. He opened the door to find a teacher handing him a letter. It was about the graduation ceremony, and Michael couldn't care less. As Michael was exiting the school, he tossed it into the garbage near the door. Michael noticed his driver waving at him, so he hopped in the limousine. Michael arrived home at almost 12PM and entered from the back door so Lisa wouldn't notice. Too bad she predicted that and welcomed him saying, "How was your exam?" She was going to her working room for a patient. As a psychiatrist, Lisa sometimes meets with her patients here in the house.

"It wasn't a big deal…" Michael responded with a sigh.

MICHAEL ENTERED his study cage as there was only one exam left, psychology. The entire reason for him taking this elective was because his mother begged him to do so. Michael dropped his stuff and studied for about five hours before having a quick nap. He woke up and made his mind about talking to his father. Michael went to his father's study room at 7:30PM, since it was the only time his father was free for his family. He isn't in a great mood around this time, but Michael had no choice. He wanted to stand up for himself; he couldn't take it anymore. Lisa was also in the room; so it was the perfect chance to talk to both.

As Michael approached the room, he heard both his parents arguing about something. Except he didn't know what the topic was. Michael opened the door without knock-ing, "Dad, mom, we need to talk."

"Ah Michael, perfect time. Come have a seat," offered Larry; he had a fake smile up his face. Michael knew that because of his psychology class. Michael sat down on the guest chair facing his mother, and on his left was Larry sitting on his fancy leather chair. Larry then changed his posture then remarked, "We found a wife for you." These words struck Michael like lighting. He froze in his place with no words to express what he was feeling now.

"What!" Michael exclaimed, and these were the only letters he could compress together.

"Your dad found a 23-year old medical student," remarked Lisa without waiting for Michael to calm down from what he heard.

"So, not only I'm being forced to get married, you want my wife to be older than me?" Michael snapped without thinking then continued, "I came here to talk to you about this. I am done with you guys taking control of my life. First, my career and now my wife, whom I'll spend my whole life with. I am 18, and I believe I can make my own decisions!"

As Michael was going to continue, Larry interrupted him and said, "Know your place! You are the son of a respected attorney, and the face of this family. You have no right to say what you just said. Not after what I've done for you since your birth. Food, education, and even entertain—" Before he could finish his sentence, Michael stood up and said "Enter-tainment you said? You locked me for more than a week and I have no friends or social life. My childhood was ruined because of you and Isabella. I wanted to be an engineer, yet you still insist on me being a judge."

With an expression that Michael had only seen once in his life when he asked them to treat him and his sister equally, Michael realized what he had done and apologized, "I'm sorry. It's just that I wanted to have a parent-son talk".

Both Larry and Lisa gazed at Michael for a moment before Lisa said, "Have a seat Michael, and tell us what's wrong". Studying psychology, Michael knew his mother would know how to open the conversation. After all, she is a psychiatrist. Michael tried to show his calm face as he sat down again. Michael took a long breath then released it. After that, he said, "All I want is to live my life like everyone else. I don't want to be moved around like a puppet, or have people choosing directions for me."

Michael stopped to take a break, but Larry thought Michael had finished. So, he explained, "As the only son of the district attorney, I have no choice but to show you to the world as what you are now. And even if you are against it, you will live your life the way I want. You have no other use than being the face of the family."

As Michael was showing a shocked face, Lisa stepped in and remarked, "Honey, enough! He is your son; at least treat him like one." Apparently, Lisa didn't agree with what Larry was doing to him; or so Michael thought. Michael believed that his mother only married Larry for his fortune.

"Listen Michael, your dad only wants what is good for you and your future. Believe me he is only treating you like this because he loves you. I'm sure Taylor is a nice girl, and you will like her," explained Lisa; yet Michael was sure that his father did not want his son's benefit but his own benefit.

Larry, on the other hand, was listening to what Lisa had to say. Then said, "Michael, I'm a busy man so I'll only say this one more time. You will marry Taylor and that's final!" Hearing those words coming out of Larry's mouth, Michael knew there was no hope in arguing with his father. Michael stood up, walked to the door, and closed the door behind him, as he was exiting. Michael was walking to his room when he overheard his parents talking. So, he stood near the door to hear.

"Nice acting, Lisa," remarked Larry.

"Thanks honey, I did what you wanted me to do," replied Lisa.

"The only reason I chose Taylor is because of her father James. He is a famous judge that has connections all over the country. I wanted Michael to marry her just so I can get closer to James." After hearing all this, Michael couldn't listen anymore. He knew before that he was being used, but he didn't know that his mother was part of it. Michael always thought of Lisa as his only shield against his father and sister. While still in shock by all what he just listened to, Michael tried to move away from the door. As he was moving, the wooden floor made a crack sound. And then he heard a yell coming from the room.

"Who is it? Come inside." Michael didn't know what to do. But thankfully, He noticed one of the butlers walking nearby. Michael told him that Larry wanted to see him now. The butler rushed to the room and entered.

After he exited, Michael asked, "What did he ask you?" The butler replied by saying, "The master asked me what I was doing near the door. I told him I was cleaning."

Somehow, Michael managed to escape from this pinch. After that, Michael went to his room, locked the door, and laid down on his bed. "I won't let my parents do what they want," he thought.

After closing his eyes for a while, Michael had already made his decision. He believed that no matter what this society thinks, money isn't always the answer. Sometimes, you need a 'free-will' in order to operate as expected. In Michael's case, the term free-will was nothing but a myth. He started to believe that it was time to stop asking and start acting. Freedom isn't something one should ask for, but rather something to fight for.

"I will escape from this hell to a better place!" muttered Michael with a grin.

ANNA

Somewhere not far from Michael's house, was the Richard's family residence. The Richard family owned a huge real-estate company that was growing rapidly. Larry and Richard were rivals since high school. Both wanted to be judges, and they even went to the same university. But things weren't always the same. Larry knew that Richard would marry the girl he loved. She was their friend since high school, but preferred Richard on Larry. Later, Richard left the university and studied abroad with his 'wife'. Since then, Larry didn't contact Richard and held grudges against him. He once even stood against him in court as the lawyer of a competitive company; but Larry lost the case.

Richard had only one child; she was named Anna. After being married for 20 years, he only had her, and no one else. Anna was a high school student who just graduated a few days ago. She wasn't tall nor was she short. She had a pixie hair-style and wore a pair of gold framed glasses. Her continuous effort to look like a boy didn't please her mother. She wanted her to be feminine while Anna believed that being a woman meant being weak.

After getting bullied a lot in middle school, mostly for being the daughter of a wealthy man, Anna changed her personality and body to create an identity for herself; and she did. All boys and girls were afraid of her and wouldn't talk to her. Although Anna knew that her colleagues hated her for not acting her gender, she couldn't care less. Because deep inside, she knows that this is the only way to survive in this society. Anna wasn't really a social person. She would always lock her door and play games or watch Anime all day. While her marks weren't the best, she still managed to keep up and graduated with an 82%. This was enough for her to enter a university at least. Although she was somewhat rich from her father, she wasted her money on games and Anime merchandise. That was another reason for her mother to be angry at her. For a while now, her mother thought that Anna was a 'mistake'. While Richard loved his only girl; her mother, on the other hand, clearly said in that she was not wanted in the house. And that she was useless as a daughter.

It had been almost two weeks after her graduation and Anna had been lying in her bed doing nothing. She didn't even take any university entry exams. After her mother insisted, Richard agreed to talk to Anna. Richard always treated his daughter like a princess. He gave her the freedom to do what her heart desired, which of course made her mother jealous. Richard went to his daughter's room and knocked on the door. The music was so loud in her room that Anna couldn't hear the outside world. After knocking a second time with no answer, Richard tried to open her door even though it was locked, he wanted to grab her attention.

Anna realized that someone was knocking on the door, so she quickly muted the music and went to unlock the door. Her kind father was smiling at her as she was opening the door.

"How can I help you dad?" asked Anna.

"I want to have a father-daughter talk with you," explained Richard, while still showing his smile.

"Sure, come in," replied Anna, as she entered her room to make space for her father.

"Actually, I want to talk to you in our special place," remarked Richard.

"Oh, all right then. It's been a while since we sat there alone," smiled Anna. Since the time she was bullied in middle school, Anna and Richard always went to their "special place". Richard would motivate her and give her solutions. Their special place was on the rooftop. They sat two chairs and a table. It was the perfect place to talk freely with only her father to listen.

The sun just sat down, and the two went to their special place. "So, Anna, how is your summer going so far?" inquired Richard.

"Great, I guess. Nothing is going on, but I'm enjoying my time," replied Anna.

"Well, I'm glad to hear that. But, did you start working on your university? Did you even choose one?" asked Richard. "Nah, it still too early. I still have time," replied Anna, as she was gazing at the sun setting. The two stopped talking for a few minutes as they were watching the sun set.

Richard then started the conversation and inquired, "By any chance, did you consider stopping watching these cartoons? I mean you are now 18, and you need to start doing your job as a grown-up woman."

"First of all," said Anna, "it's called 'Anime'; and I won't stop. Also, what do you mean by 'job'? What do I have to do?" Richard took a breath then explained, "For instance, take care of your body, search for a university, and clean your room. You just need to be more responsible."

"I guess you are right. But still, I believe that I'm fine with the current me. I don't need to change," remarked Anna, while fixing her glasses that slipped.

Shortly after both were silent, Rita appeared behind them and said, "I was calling you for a while now. Haven't thought that you would be in this place. Anyway, dinner is ready."

"Honey, what did I tell you about not coming here? This is a special place for me and Anna," remarked Richard, as he and Anna were standing up.

"Yeah, whatever, just hurry and come to the dining room," said Rita, as she walked back inside.

The family sat at the long table, with their food being served by the cook. They were having a peaceful dinner, before Rita stared at Anna and said, "So, did you pick a university or not?" Anna swallowed the piece of chicken she just ate then said, "No I haven't," as she ate another piece.

"You do realize that you have almost no time left. Why don't you just enter the same university as my friend's daughter?" said Rita with a full mouth.

"Who, Sophia? No way, I hate that girl. She is a girl who wasn't raised well by her parents." Rita smacked her fork on the table and snarled "What did you just say? Don't you dare insult her parents! You are the one who wasn't raised well." Hearing those words come out of her mother's mouth, Anna placed her fork on the table, stood up, and went to her room without saying a single word.

"Honey, don't you think that you overreacted on such a stupid thing?" asked Richard as he continued to enjoy his food. "Damn it!" snapped Rita as she hit the table with her fist.

It was not until this moment that Rita knew what to do with her daughter. She finished her meal and then told Richard that she had something to do. Rita changed her clothes and called her friend. She whispered to her friend something, then headed out through the back door. Anna, on the other hand, was in her room reading a new Manga she just bought that day. Richard went to his library to relax for a while.

"Sorry for meeting you at such a short notice," apologized Rita to her friend, Olivia, who was meeting with her at a café. "It all right, I had nothing to do for the night. Anyway, what did you want to talk with me about?" inquired Olivia.

"I want you to help me get rid of my daughter." Explained Rita while showing a serious face. "Are you insane? You want to get rid of your only daughter?" snapped Olivia.

"I just can't take her actions anymore. She is useless at the house, a free loader to be more specific. But since her father loves her more than me, I need to change his view on her," remarked Rita after sipping from her coffee.

"Do you have any plans in mind?" asked Olivia.

"That's why I called you, I want to accuse her of something that will make even her father turn against her," replied Rita.

"Hmm, something to accuse her with," said Olivia while thinking. After almost three minutes of silence, Olivia snapped and said, "How about planting drugs in her bedroom? I know people who can give me some… But it's too extreme, never mind what I just said."

Rita immediately exclaimed, "Actually, that's an awesome idea. I might just do that." Olivia knew this was a bad idea and asked, "Are you sure? This could cause a lot of trouble between her and her father."

Rita replied by saying, "Which is exactly what I want."

"If you insist then I have no problem," said Olivia after losing hope in convincing her otherwise.

"Then it's settled. I'll meet later to discuss furthermore. For now, check with your friend about how to get some drugs," said Rita. "Will do," replied Olivia.

They then changed the subject and talked for a while. Olivia was surprised of how cold-hearted her friend was. "It's getting late, I need to return. Otherwise Richard will start worrying," said Rita as she stood up.

"Sure, see you later," said Olivia. Since Olivia hasn't eaten all her food, she stayed behind while Rita returned home.

Rita entered the home at about 9:45PM and then went to have a cool shower before joining her husband in bed. On the other side of the house, Anna was in her room lying on her bed. Thinking about what her mother just said; she was just confused. "How could my mother prefer that girl and her family over me?" thought Anna. She slowly closed her eyes. And after a while, she fell asleep without changing to her sleeping dress.

IT WAS 8:00AM, Anna just realized that she had slept the entire night with her clothes on, and the lights turned on. She changed her clothes and then went to the bathroom to do her morning routine. She then went downstairs to eat her break-fast alongside her father who was late for work.

"Morning Dad," said Anna. "Morning Anna," replied Richard. He had just finished eating his breakfast. So, he rushed to his car. Anna sat down at the table as the cook was cooking her breakfast.

"There you go," said the cook.

"Thanks," replied Anna.

After eating her breakfast, Anna went to her room to prepare. She wanted to head out and smell some fresh air. At almost 9:30AM, Anna exited her house and went with the driver to find a nice place for walking.

FATE

IT'D BEEN A DAY SINCE MICHAEL HAD THAT CONVERSATION WITH his parents. He had already made his decision to leave this greedy family. The problem was that Michael had nowhere to go. And he couldn't live on his own, not after living this luxurious life. He will need a perfect plan. Michael only has one exam remaining, plus the graduation ceremony. After that, he'll have a long summer holiday; perfect for escaping. Michael needs to stay calm during these few days and wear his poker face. For now, Michael had to revise for his exam tomorrow, and then sleep at the same time as always just to be less suspicious.

Michael woke up at 7:30AM. He loves waking up early, even during holidays. A time when his sister is sleeping and sometimes his parent are still asleep. Michael went to the bathroom to do his morning routine. After taking a cool shower and brushing his teeth, he returned to his room and found a breakfast tray waiting near the door. Michael enjoys eating his meals away from his family. While eating breakfast, Michael read through the whole notes he took in the class. At

8:00AM Michael packed his stuff and went to the limousine which was waiting for him outside.

Michael entered the school and had some time before the exam started. So, he sat in the place that had his name written on it. Michael tried to close his eyes for a moment of relaxation, but he soon realized that you couldn't do that when you are the top student at school. In a blink, a group of students surrounded him to ask questions. Michael stood up at once and said, "Sorry guys, I gotta go to the toilet before the exam starts."

He rushed to the toilet and locked himself in to have a peaceful moment before the exam. Michael was enjoying his time until he glanced at his watch, it was 8:45AM. "This doesn't look good. The exam started five minutes ago," muttered Michael as he ran back to the class.

"Sorry for being late, I went to the toilet," Michael explained while catching his breath after running.

"Ugh, it's you again. Fine, start your exam; but you won't get any extra time," remarked Jimmy. He just hates Michael; and he had only taught him once two years ago. But up till now, Jimmy could not accept anyone being 'smarter than him'. So, after Michael was the only student Jimmy had taught to get an A+, Jimmy started being rude to Michael and tell lies about him to other teachers. Never mind him, Michael sat on his chair and flipped through the exam papers.

He peaked quickly at all the questions then muttered, "25... In 25 minutes I'll finish the exam." Jimmy heard him and snapped, "25 minutes you say? Don't be ridiculous, the exam was created to be solved in an hour."

"Is that so?" challenged Michael as he was wrapping up the first paper.

After almost 25 minutes, Michael stood up, went to Jimmy's desk, slowly placed the paper on his table, and left the exam room.

"Wait!" yelled Jimmy. Michael was already closing the door behind him. Michael called his driver, who was waiting for him outside. He entered the car then heard the driver in front saying, "That was fast, like really fast."

"Well, it's not a big deal after all."

On the way home, Michael tried to brainstorm some ideas for his escape. He will probably need a servant to work with him behind the scenes. "Most likely, it will be David. He is the only one I can share this plan with. Of course, I won't tell him the exact plan, in case something happens," thought Michael.

After arriving, and while David was opening the door for him, Michael asked, "Hey David, can I ask you something?"

"Yeah sure, what's on your mind?" replied David showing his usual smile.

"Can I trust you enough to share something special and very important to me with you?" asked Michael while narrowing his eyes. "Um, I guess so," answered David.

"I see, then I'll talk to you later; most likely in a week or so," remarked Michael while heading to the villa entrance.

"Sure," noted David and drove to park the limousine.

Michael entered the house, and as usual he found Lisa standing in front of him. She doesn't know that Michael already knew what was behind her "motherly" mask. "So, how was your day Michael? Did you ace that psychology exam?" asked Lisa with a smile, that just a while ago, Michael knew was fake. "It was easy; don't worry," replied Michael as he passed Lisa and went to his room.

It was almost 9AM, Michael sat down at his desk and

powered his computer to check the school website. Since Michael threw the graduation ceremony paper, he had to search the school website for the ceremony information, such as the place and time. Although Michael never intended to go, he is now forced to go because Larry will give a speech as the district attorney.

Michael sent the information to both his parents' e-mail. He then changed his school uniform to his everyday clothes and went out of the house. Whenever Michael wanted to have some quality time with himself or just to get out of the family environment, he would go to the local zoo. It wasn't that far away, almost 10 minutes by bike. Before heading out, Michael grabbed his small bag, and put in a notebook, a phone charger and a bottle of water.

Michael arrived at the zoo. And since it was still early in the morning, most children were in school. So, the zoo was empty, just how he liked it. Michael walked through the animals while brainstorming in his mind. After the graduation ceremony, he will need to think about his future. Which university to enroll in? And since he is escaping, Michael needed to find a university in the country he was going to... but where? Michael rested his bike by a bench and then sat down near the crow's cage. Michael loves crows; he wouldn't mind staring at them for hours. Their sound helps him relax and think clearly. Michael took out his small notebook and started writing anything that popped up in his mind. Still, he feels that something is missing. But what is it? After zoning out for a while Michael fell asleep without noticing. He felt something cold and wet touching his hands; it was raining.

~

MEANWHILE, Anna was at the same zoo walking when it started to rain. She was heading to her driver who was waiting in the parking zone. Anna was glad that she brought an umbrella with her. As she was searching for the exit, she found someone sitting on a bench without moving. Anna approached him as she was wondering why he wasn't taking shield from the rain.

Michael, who was spattered with raindrops all over his body, dreamt about being cornered by a rain storm. He was almost swallowed by the storm. Anna reached him and then saw a boy soaked with rain. She took her umbrella and held it above Michaels's head to cover him. Suddenly, Michael's dream vanished. He saw the storm disappearing as the sun rose. Michael then gently opened his eyes to see the real world. He noticed a girl who he thought was a boy, then saw the umbrella protecting him from the rain. "If you sleep under the rain, you will catch a cold for sure," remarked Anna.

Michael snapped and knew she was a girl. Michael noticed his soaked notebook and quickly shoved it into his small bag. "Who are you?" he asked. Over the years, and with all the challenges he faced; Michael started to have trust issues. He doesn't trust anyone at all, not even his parents. "I'm Anna from the Richard family."

"Do you have someone to drive you home?" she then asked.

"Actually, I came here using this bike," answered Michael while pointing at his bike.

"Oh, I see. Then I guess you can come with me. I have my driver waiting for me near the entrance," offered Anna.

"Is it all right? I mean I'm soaked with water, and I have a bike," inquired Michael.

"No problem. The car is big enough to fit you and your bike," she replied with a smile.

Michael stood from his place and carried his bag while walking beside his bike. Anna offered him to join her under the umbrella, but Michael hated the idea since he didn't trust her. While walking, Anna stopped and asked, "By the way, what is your name?"

"My name is Michael," Michael answered as he continued to drag his bike beside him.

"Michael huh, what a nice name," remarked Anna. "Is your house near the zoo?" she asked.

"Ah, yes; it is a ten-minute ride by bike," he explained.

"So, it isn't so far," noted Anna.

The two walked for about five minutes before reaching the gate. Anna then called her driver to bring the car to the gate. Anna entered first while the driver and Michael were putting the bike in the trunk. "So, where do you live?" asked Anna.

"Brierley Glen Avenue," answered Michael while drying himself.

"You mean that Brierley Glen? How did your family manage to buy a house there? Only the richest people could afford it," inquired Anna.

"Well, you see," said Michael, "My dad is Los Angeles' district attorney."

"What did you just say, a district attorney? You are so lucky to live in such a family," remarked Anna.

"Actually, I'm not," replied Michael with a sigh.

"What do you mean?" asked Anna.

"It's, nothing," hesitated Michael; he couldn't tell her his true intention. Michael wanted to change the subject, so he took the towel off his head then and asked, "What about you Anna? Your parents are also rich."

"I guess you are right," replied Anna while smiling.

Michael arrived at his house. The rain had stopped by then, and the sun was shining again. "All right then, thanks for letting me come with you," remarked Michael as he opened the car door.

"Wait!" snapped Anna. She then wrote something on a piece of paper. "Here, take this," offered Anna while giving Michael the paper.

Michael took the paper not knowing its contents. He then closed the door and saw Anna waving at him as the car started to move. Michael hid the paper in his pocket and entered the house.

It was still eleven in the morning, and Michael had nothing to do. He went up to his room, changed his clothes, and then lay on his bed thinking about what happened in the park. Michael then remembered the piece of paper that Anna gave him. After taking it from his old pants and opened it, Michael examined it. "A number? Why would she give me a number?" thought Michael.

He placed the paper on the table near his bed and then closed his eyes. Suddenly Michael snapped; it was then that he remembered that he had forgotten his bike in the car.

ENVY

Michael reached for his phone and tried to dial the number Anna gave him. The phone rang once, then twice, but still no response. As Michael was about to hang up the phone, he heard a voice saying, "Hello."

Michael immediately replied "Um, Anna?"

"That's me. So, you called."

"Well, actually I called just to tell you that I forgot my bike in your car," explained Michael.

"Oh, I see. Can you come to my house to pick it up?" replied Anna.

"Um... sure, why not? Where do you live?" asked Michael.

"I'll text you the address," said Anna, and then continued, "All right, see you soon I guess."

Michael hung up the call, then dressed up. He waited for the address that Anna was supposed to send by now. Michael called David and told him to prepare the car. Then they went to the address written. After driving for 15 minutes, they were finally able to reach Anna's house. Michael stood out of the car and went to ring the bell. The door opened, it was Anna.

"Oh, it's you, just give me a second, I'll bring your bike," said Anna, and then went inside.

"There you go," she handed Michael his bike.

"Thanks," replied Michael.

"So, I was wondering, do you wanna have coffee or something?" asked Anna.

Michael was shocked; he didn't know what to say. Plus, he didn't know her, not to mention trust her. "Um…" Michael hesitated then stopped for a while before continuing, "Sure why not. But not today, I'm busy."

"It's alright, we can decide on a day later," said Anna, and then continued, "I'll contact you later."

Michael took his bike and went to his car. As he was walking, he flicked his eyes just to see Anna's face once more. She was waving at him before she closed the door. Michael was just confused; he just agreed to drink coffee with a girl he doesn't really know.

Anna returned to her house to find her mother waiting for her. "Who was that?" asked Rita, with a serious face. "It's no one," answered Anna.

"Don't play dumb with me. I said who was outside," shouted Rita.

Anna calmly sighed then said, "Someone who lost his bike, and I found it for him. He just came to pick it up."

"Is that so?" said Rita. Anna didn't want this conversation to be any longer. So, she walked past her mother and said, "Sorry gotta go."

Rita watched her daughter going upstairs. Rita started to believe that it was time to end this between her and Anna. She then called Olivia and said, "Olivia, any news on the... you know..." Olivia tried to convince her one last time, "Are you sure you want to do this?" she asked.

"Yes, Olivia, I'm sure. Now, did you get the stuff?" inquired Rita.

"Yes, I did. I'll meet you tonight at 9PM if that's okay with you," offered Olivia.

"Sure, it's all right, then we will meet at the place we agreed on," remarked Rita.

"All right then, see you soon."

As for Michael, he had to go with his father to buy clothes for the graduation ceremony which was in about one week. Michael was reading his book when his father knocked at his door. "Come on, it's time to go," he said.

"I'm coming," replied Michael as he placed the book on the table and took his stuff before opening the door.

"Let's go, we're already late. It's almost five." noted Larry.

They went to a tailor that Larry knew for a while. On their way, Larry asked Michael, "Did you choose a university yet? Keep in mind that I won't allow you to enroll in any random one. I know a good law school in case you haven't chosen yet."

Michael knows that he will not join a university here, but the country he is escaping to, which he still had to decide on. "Dad as I told you before I don't want to be a judge, I studied to be an engineer," argued Michael.

"This again? I told you that I don't want to go through this again. You are my successor and will be a judge. And if you don't want to choose a university, I'll force you into it," demanded Larry.

It was 6:30PM, and the two had just finished with the tailor. On the way back home, no one spoke to the other. After parking, Michael got out of the car and went to his room. He got a message on his phone. It was a strange number. The message read: "Hi, it's me, Anna. So, about our conversation today, did you decide on a time that will fit you?"

"Just how many numbers does she have?" thought Michael as he was sending her his answer. "First of all, why do you have two numbers? What about the first one?" he texted, then sent another message, "And I believe tomorrow is fine by me," sent Michael.

Moments later, Anna responded, "Delete the first number. I bought this number secretly so that I can talk to you without my parents knowing. Ever since they knew that you are from Larry's family, they forbade me from talking to you." Anna continued, "I'm free tomorrow all day. How about nine in the morning?" Just now, Michael remembered the rivalry between Larry and Anna's father. Michael used to hear stories about them when they were in high school. Although Michael knew he would be in big trouble if his parents found out about his relation, he wanted to risk it all.

"Are you still here?" sent Anna. Michael woke out of his imaginary world, and quickly sent, "Yeah sure, nine sounds good for me."

"Then it's settled, tomorrow nine. I'll meet you at the café near the zoo. By the way, do you have a driving license?" sent Anna.

"Yes, I do," replied Michael.

"Good, then drive to the café alone without telling your parents. This is the only possible way," texted Anna.

Michael closed the phone when he heard someone knocking his door.

"Your dinner, Sir," spoke the cook. Michael opened the door to take his tray. "Thanks for the food," he smiled, before closing the door behind him.

He bolted through dinner then laid the tray in front of his door, for the butler to pick up. Michael then went to his entertainment room. It's been a while since he went there. Michael grabbed a random book from the huge library and started reading.

Meanwhile, his parents were discussing the marriage. "Have you finished the arrangements for the wedding?" asked Lisa, as she was sipping a cup of white tea. "Don't worry, I have everything under control. But, when do you think is the best day for the wedding?" asked Larry.

"Hmm... let's see. I believe the week after the graduation ceremony is our best choice. How about a Friday?" recommended Lisa.

"Yeah, Friday would be great?" Larry stopped then continued, "Anyway, remember to tell Michael about the wedding details, and keep your act going," said Larry with a grin.

"No need to tell me that. I'll make sure that Michael has the best wedding."

The two continued talking as they drank their cup of tea.

IT WAS 8:45PM, and Rita was getting ready to meet Olivia.

She put on her black coat and wore her beanie. "Alright honey, I'm going to meet my friend. Eat without me," she said.

"Which friend?" inquired Richard.

"Olivia. You know her," replied Rita.

"Oh, that Olivia. Anyway, don't be late. You know how the streets get after nine," added Richard.

Rita exited the house after making sure Anna couldn't see her. Rita drove for around 15 minutes before reaching the place. It was already 9:10PM when Rita approached Olivia from behind and tapped her shoulder. Olivia shrieked, "You scared me." She then took a breath before continuing, "You're late. You know that I hate standing in these dark allies at night."

"Sorry, I lost track of time, while convincing Richard. Never mind that, you brought it?" asked Rita.

"Yup, right here," answered Olivia while pointing at her purse. Olivia shoved her hand quickly into the brown purse and grabbed a small pack. "Open your bag quickly," trembled Olivia, with her hands shaking.

"Easy now, no need to worry that much," remarked Rita, as she opened her small handbag.

"What do you mean 'no need to worry'? We are doing a crime," barked Olivia.

After the operation finished, Rita walked away from Olivia and toward her car. She turned her head and said, "Thanks Olivia, I owe you one."

Then each woman went her own way. Rita returned home and found Richard alongside Anna eating their dinner. "You are so early what happened?" asked Richard, with his mouth full.

"Olivia received an urgent call, so she had to cancel our dinner," explained Rita.

"Do you wanna have dinner with us? It's not late, I can tell the cook to bring you something?" inquired Richard.

"No, I'm fine."

Anna was sitting on the other side of the table across Rita, who had just arrived. She finished her dinner, then went to her room to prepare for the next day.

ANNA WOKE up from the beeping of her alarm clock. She was motivated to start this day. She went to her bathroom to brush her teeth and wear her clothes. She hasn't told anyone about her so-called date; yet, her mother spotted her leaving the house. Rita thought that this was the best opportunity to plant the drugs. It was a Wednesday, and Richard had an urgent meeting with his company. So, he went out at 7:30AM, while Anna was still asleep. And now, the house was clear for Rita to proceed with her plan. She made sure that the butler, and the cook were downstairs and had work to do. Rita entered Anna's room carelessly. She struggled to reach the desk as the floor was filled with random stuff. Rita messed around for a moment to think of a perfect place for an 18-year old girl to hide her drugs! Rita finally snapped, she found the perfect place, Anna's library.

"I'll stash it inside a fake book cover," Rita thought before hurrying to the stationery store near them. She bought a fake book stash and then returned to Anna's room. Rita noticed the butler entering Anna's bedroom. She hurried in then ordered, "Wait, don't clean now."

"But Anna told me to clean her room," replied the innocent butler.

Rita thought for a second before saying, "She just called me. She wants you to clean her room after she returns."

"Yes, madam," responded the butler before walking away from Anna's bedroom. Rita locked the door behind her and then opened the fake book. She stashed the entire package she got from Olivia inside the book. Rita then placed the book smoothly between Anna's other books. Looking at the library from a distance, it will seem like a normal one. But, once you look closely, you will find a stash full of drugs. Rita quickly exited the room as she didn't want to leave anything behind her. She went to the dining room to have breakfast. After all, Rita hadn't eaten anything since last night. She was busy planting drugs in her daughter's bedroom. Now, Rita needs to play the waiting game. She was the predator waiting for her prey to approach the trap so that she can assault.

DISGRACE

WHILE RITA WAS CELEBRATING THE SUCCESS OF HER PLAN, Anna arrived at the café; she entered and looked around trying to find Michael. Anna then checked her mobile clock, and it was 9:05AM. She then heard a voice from behind, "Over here." Michael whispered. Anna barely heard him. She turned around to find Michael sitting near the window while holding a book. Anna approached him, then sat on the opposite chair.

"Was I late?" She inquired.

"No, I came here early since I had nothing to do at home," Michael placed his book inside his slang bag. He then asked, "Wanna drink something?" he was trying not to meet her gaze.

"Yeah, I didn't have any breakfast," laughed Anna. She then went to the counter to order something to eat. Meanwhile, Michael zoned out. He was daydreaming when Anna asked, "Did you order anything?"

Michael snapped and said, "Ah, yes I ordered a cup of coffee." Anna sat down in her place as she was waiting for her order to be prepared. "So, how was your day?" asked Anna, while showing a bright smile on her face. For a moment, Michael blushed; he then shook his head. He reminded himself that he didn't trust her yet. And so, Michael reclaimed his usual face and replied, "Nothing special. Same usual morning, but with no school." Michael stopped for a second then asked, "What about you? How was your day?"

"Good, I guess." Both were silent as no one knew what to say. Later, Anna stood up and said, "Looks like my order is ready." She went to receive her order while Michael sat in his place thinking about his future.

Anna finished her breakfast. Michael was just staring at her while shifting his gaze whenever she looked back at him. Suddenly, a phone started to ring; it was Michael's, and the caller was his mother. "Excuse me for a second," he then walked away from the table and tapped the answer icon on his phone.

"Hello, Michael. Where are you? I was worried since you didn't eat breakfast with us," inquired Lisa.

"I went to a cafe and ate breakfast there. Just a change of routine," replied Michael.

"Oh, I see. Anyway, next time you must tell either your dad or me. We were worried that something had happened to you," ordered Lisa. "Don't worry mom, I'm fine. I'll return home soon. Also, don't save me breakfast," remarked Michael, before hanging up the phone.

"Did something happen?" inquired Anna. Michael sat down then replied, "No, it was my mom. She was trying to sound like a caring mother." Michael stopped talking. He realized what he had just said.

"Ah, do not worry. It's nothing," gulped Michael. Anna

snickered, and Michael blushed again. She then stood up, "All right then, I think I need to return home before my parents notice my absence."

"I'll stay here for a while."

"Ok, we'll stay in touch," said Anna, as she was heading toward the exit. Michael grabbed his book from the bag and resumed from where he stopped last. Little did Anna know about what awaited her back home…

ANNA ARRIVED home and parked her car. She walked in and went directly to her room, before hearing a knock on the door. "Yes?"

"It's me," replied Rita.

Anna quickly opened the door. Rita was showing her spooky face when she said, "Where have you been?" Anna calmly replied, "I was eating breakfast at the café near us."

"Is that so? Well, next time tell us where you are going," demanded Rita.

"Well it's not like you were worried or anything," said Anna with a plain face. "What did you say—" Before Rita could finish her sentence, Anna grabbed the doorknob then said, "Anyway, I have stuff I need to finish. So, see you later I guess," she then closed the door, with Rita on the other side.

Rita was about to go berserk, but then remembered that it was only a matter of time before Anna would be grounded by Richard. Rita calmed herself and then went to her room. She only went to Anna's room to make sure that Anna hadn't noticed the fake book.

Around lunchtime, Richard returned. Rita welcomed him

home while being in a great mood. Richard felt something was strange then asked, "What's with that mood? You seem more excited than usual."Rita smiled then said, "Let's just say that I'm looking forward to something."

"I see. By the way, I'm starving. What's for lunch?" inquired Richard.

"It's your favorite, burger steak."

"All right then, I'll go change my clothes."

As Richard was headed for his room, he passed by Anna's room. He knocked the door and said, "How was your day sweetie?"

"As always, Dad. Nothing new, I guess," answered Anna, as she was watching an Anime show. She was wearing her head-phones, which she removed the moment Richard knocked on the door.

"Lunch is ready, come eat with us," remarked Richard.

"Sorry Dad, I'm busy. Can you tell the butler to bring my dish upstairs?"

"As you wish, but keep in mind that we love to eat with our daughter," stated Richard, then went to his room to change his clothes.

MICHAEL RETURNED HOME SHORTLY AFTERWARDS, he told the cook to bring lunch to up to his room, as his parents had already eaten theirs. After eating lunch, Michael felt dizzy and wanted to sleep for an hour or so. He sat an alarm to wake him after an hour and then switched off the lights. Michael closed his eyes for five minutes before Isabella marched in his room and opened the lights.

"Wake up, mom told me to go with you to the supermarket."

Michael rubbed his eyes then said, "Can't you see that I'm trying to sleep? Plus, don't you have school today?"

"Actually, school finished," barked Isabella.

"Can't you go with David?" asked Michael.

"No, mom said he has work to do."

"Fine, fine. Just wait for me outside," demanded Michael, as he was walking towards the door to close it. Michael just couldn't understand why Isabella gets all the attention, and why does her demands always got yes for an answer. He changed his clothes in a hurry and then went to his waiting sister outside. "All right let's go," yawned Michael.

Both exited the mansion; Michael was riding the bike while Isabella sat behind him. They went to the nearby supermarket. Michael was tired, so he didn't even bother entering the market, so he waited outside for his sister. The two then went back home while Michael's parents were waiting for him to talk.

Michael entered the house after Isabella as he was storing his bike. When he entered, he heard his mother calling, "Michael, come to your father's study room." Michael immediately knew that nothing good would happen in there. He went to his room to change his clothes and then went to Larry's room. Michael knocked on the door before entering the room. As usual, he found his father at his desk, and his mother sitting on the other side. Just like last time. "Close the door behind you," ordered Larry. Michael closed the door, then walked to his seat and sat slowly on it.

"Your father and I talked. And we decided to host the wedding a week after your graduation ceremony. Friday, to be more precise," Lisa said. Michael sat still and didn't say anything.

"We have contacted Taylor's family, and they have no problem with that date. Also, tomorrow Taylor and her parents are coming here for dinner," stated Larry.

"Is that all?" inquired Michael. It was obvious to his psychiatrist mother that Michael had no interest in the conversation whatsoever."Honey, regarding what your father just said, you will need to dress well for tomorrow to make a good impression on Taylor and her parents. You got that?" explained Lisa.

"Yes, I got it. Now, since we're done here, I would like you to excuse me," Michael spoke, while standing up and heading towards the door. He now had a target for his goal, "The night before the wedding, huh. So basically, I have almost 15 days to plan," thought Michael.

ANNA SLID her empty dish tray near her door and then locked herself in her cave. She dressed and prepared to go to her soon-to-be university. Richard told Anna to at least check a few universities as some offer an "open day" for potential students. She believed that there is no need to go as she had already decided which university to choose. Anna walked by Richard, who was heading for his study room. "Going to university?" inquired Richard.

"Yup…" Answered Anna, then continued, "for now, I'm just gonna check this new campus that was built near our neighborhood."

"All right then, good luck," smiled Richard.

Anna took off. It was almost an 8-minute drive to the university. While she was driving, she just remembered something. Anna forgot to lock her room when she left. Anna always locked her door whenever she would leave. That way she could lock her secrets away from her parents. After calming herself down, Anna thought, "Perhaps, just perhaps, no one will realize that the door is unlocked." Speaking of the devil, her phone rang. It was her father. But since Anna was driving, Richard was reconnected with the voice mail.

"I hope you're not busy now. I just wanted to ask about that book I lent you before, the one about the 'Alpha Real-estate Project'. My client needs it, so please call me when you're free."

"Now what? The book is in my room. I forgot it in my shelf," thought Anna.

After arriving at the university, and thinking about it, Anna concluded that she had no choice but to tell Richard where the book was. She grabbed her phone out of her bag and then dialed her father's number. "Hello, Anna?" spoke Richard.

"Dad, sorry I was driving. And about the book, I believe it's in my shelf. My door is unlocked," she remarked. Richard was in a hurry, so he quickly said, "All right sweetie - thanks," then ended the call. Anna entered the campus as Richard was entering her room. Yet this time, she wouldn't be around as always.

Meanwhile, as Richard was approaching Anna's shelf, Rita was in her bedroom waiting for the big news. Richard combed the shelves till he found the book. As he was about to leave, his eyes locked on a strange book. It didn't look like a normal book. Richard grabbed the book out of curiosity and felt something was wrong. The book was too light for its size. He then noticed that this wasn't an ordinary book. Richard tried to open it, and it was a shock. Rita, who was in the next room, heard something falling. She then hurried to Anna's room, showing a utterly shocked face, while deep inside, it was quite the opposite…

IGNOMINY

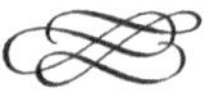

"WHAT HAPPENED?" ASKED RITA SHOWING HER FAKE SHOCKED face.

"O-O-OUR daughter," stuttered Richard.

"What about her?" inquired Rita, as she was approaching Richard from behind.

"My daughter, she… she…" Richard just couldn't express what he had just found. Rita came from behind and noticed the book. "Oh my god! Is that what I think it is?" shouted Rita.

"Rita, our daughter is an ADDICT!" cried Richard. Never in his life, had Richard revealed this face; a face full of tears, regret and anger. His only daughter, whom he loved more than anything, is an addict. Richard didn't realize that giving his daughter her freedom meant she would take this route.

"What should we do?" asked Rita, with tears on her face. She wiped the tears then continued, "I noticed that Anna's behavior had changed. But I thought it was puberty. I didn't think she was hiding such thing in her bedroom. But now it makes sense, the isolation, and locking her door."

Richard couldn't process anything now. He took the stash

and went to his study room. He locked the door behind him as Rita was enjoying her victory deep inside herself.

Anna had finished what she came for and was headed back home. It was already 10pm, past dinnertime. Anna parked her car and then opened the door to find two hopeless faces waiting for her. "Mom? Dad? What's going on?" Both Rita and Richard stayed silent. Until Rita broke the silence and stated, "We found it, Anna."

"I don't get it? What did you find?" replied Anna, with an innocent face. It was then that Richard exploded and roared, "Don't play dumb on your parents. We found the drugs that you hid in the stash."Anna was showing a puzzled face. She had absolutely no idea of what her parents were talking about.

"Drugs? What drugs? I swear that I don't know what you're talking about," begged Anna.

"Come with me," dictated Richard, as he grabbed Anna's hand to his study room. "How about now?" asked Richard, as he was holding the book.

"I have never seen this book in my life," insisted Anna.

While Anna was dealing with her father, she saw Rita behind him showing an evil smile with deep piercing eyes. It was at this moment that Anna realized something was going on.

"Dad, please believe me. I don't do drugs; I never did!" sobbed Anna. At this point, she was desperate. She didn't know how to react, nor how to defend herself against her sneering father.

"Do you know what, I don't have time to waste on you. Tomorrow morning we'll have you tested. That way we can make sure once and for all," stated Richard. He tried to inhale and exhale, just to calm himself down. Richard then looked sharply at his daughter, then ordered, "Go to your room now. And be ready by 9AM tomorrow."

Rita tried to spice things up, "What about your meeting tomorrow morning?"

"I don't care, I need to know whether my daughter is clean or not," responded Richard then left the room and went to his bedroom.

Rita then followed, looking one last time at Anna. This time, she made sure that Anna could see her deep eyes. The room was empty. Anna knelt on her knees, and tears started to slide down her cheeks.

After almost five minutes, Anna stood up and went upstairs to her bedroom. She was tired, confused, and kind on angry. "How could my dad claim things without any evidence? I'm almost certain that someone planted the drugs, but who? The most suspicious one is my mom. But, why would she do such a thing?" wondered Anna in tears. She was lying on her bed when Michael flashed in her mind. Anna quickly took her phone that was on the table near her. She called Michael. For Anna, she believed that the only one who could help her was Michael.

The phone rang once, twice, thrice; Anna knew that it was almost midnight, so she gave up. As she was reaching for the end call icon, she heard a voice. "Hello. Anna?" muttered Michael. He glanced at his clock - it was 11:30pm.

"Michael, sorry for calling at this time," sobbed Anna.

"What going on? Something happened?" snapped Michael.

"Yes, please can you meet me in the park?" begged Anna. "You mean that park?" inquired Michael. He was now fully awake.

"Yes, I'll wait for you there," whispered Anna. She then quickly ended the call.

MICHAEL PUT on his clothes and quietly exited the house from behind. He then hopped on his bike. Along the way, Michael was thinking about what could have happened to Anna that she would call him at 11PM. He arrived at the park and started to look for Anna. After walking around for a while, he found a short-haired woman sitting on a bench. It was her, no doubt about it. Michael approached her slowly until he could clearly see her face. When he made sure it was Anna, he sat down beside her. "Thanks for coming Michael," said Anna while wiping her tears.

"It's all right. Anyway, what happened?" asked Michael.

"Someone stashed drugs in my room. My dad found them, and now he is accusing me," explained Anna. Then continued, "And tomorrow my dad is going to test me for drugs. I don't know why anyone one would do something like this. I guess I'm not wanted in the family anymore."

Michael was shocked and didn't know what to say. He didn't know if Anna was telling the truth or not. Still, since she came to him at this time, He tried to keep up with her and asked, "I doubt anyone in your family would do such a thing."

"Actually, I started to notice that my mom has something on me. I don't know why, probably because of the way I am now. I bet she wanted me to act my gender. Anyway, I made up my mind; I want to escape this family. If they won't accept me for who I am, then I'll just leave them."

Suddenly, Michael snapped. A light bulb flashed in his

head. He then faced Anna and said, "Actually, I didn't tell you. But I am planning on escaping."

"What! Why would someone who is living such a life want to escape?" inquired Anna.

"It's not about how I live. It's about the price I have to pay; my freedom," remarked Michael. Michael then told Anna about the life he was living in that house. How he is forced to marry someone and enroll in a major he doesn't like. Anna was astonished by what Michael had told her. She realized that both had the same goal and so she asked, "Then, how about we both escape together?"

Michael closed his eyes for a moment. "She could hold me back. And I don't need another person to accompany me. Also, I don't trust her," all these thoughts were swimming in Michael's mind. He then took a deep breath in, then exhaled. After that, he slowly opened his eyes and said, "I'll ask you again. Are you sure that you want to go with me? Knowing that you might regret it later?"

"Yes, I'm sure. I have nowhere to stay after all. We can enroll in any university and continue our life anywhere else," explained Anna. While Michael still had his mind on her, he kind of felt sorry for her. "Then it's settled; you will come with me. But, try to act normally for the next few weeks," spoke Michael. Anna gained her smiley face back; she felt relieved. "Ok, what exactly do I have to do?" she asked.

"First, the wedding is going to take place the week after my graduation. It will be on a Friday, we need to be ready by the night before the wedding," explained Michael, and then added, "Tomorrow Taylor, my fiancé, will come for dinner at my place. We need to meet at noon, or after your drug test. There I'll tell you the in-depth details about the plan. For now, you return home, and act normal. Your parents will probably keep an eye on you. Try not to grab attention."

"I'll do my best. Again, I'm sorry for dragging you into my problem. I really appreciate it. I'll be on my way, I guess. See you tomorrow," said Anna, while standing up.

"Sure, see you tomorrow," Michael was still sitting in his place as he saw Anna disappear into the dark. "This is gonna be tough," hr thought to himself.

Michael returned home and made sure no one saw him leaving or entering. He went to his room, changed his clothes, and went to bed. He watched his clock, and it was 12:30AM. Michael closed his eyes and tried to resume his sleep.

"MICHAEL, honey? Are you still sleeping? It's 9AM already!" said Lisa, as she was knocking on his door.

Michael snapped and glared at his clock. "I overslept. Well, I can't be blamed. After what happened last night, I'm still sleepy," thought Michael. He opened his door at once, "Your breakfast is downstairs. Come and eat. And what's with your face? You look pale," remarked Lisa.

"It's nothing, I was up late yesterday reading," replied Michael.

"Is that so? Anyway, you need to be fresh for today's special dinner," stated Lisa.

Michael went downstairs to eat. "Come to think of it. Anna should be on her way to get tested for drugs by now," thought Michael.

~

"COME ON ANNA, we're late. Are you still sleeping?" Barked Richard, as he was knocking rapidly on Anna's door.

Anna quickly got out of bed and said, "No, I was wearing my clothes. Give me a minute."

"I'll wait in my car," he snarked, marching off.

Anna tried to calm herself as she knew that the test would have no effect. After all, she was already clean to start with. The Richard family went to a lab Richard knew. There, Anna was put to a quick drug check. Obviously, it was negative; Anna was clean. Richard was shocked, yet relieved that his daughter wasn't an addict. Still, he had no idea how that drug ended up in Anna's room. Rita, on the other hand, knew that Anna was clean. She then tried to act relieved in front of Richard.

The family were heading home, when Richard spoke, "Even though the test showed that you are clean. The fact that you hid drugs in your room—" Anna interrupted and insisted, "I told you, I didn't know about the drugs."

Richard adjusted the rearview mirror so that his eyes could meet Anna's. He then said, "I don't care, from now on, things will change. First, you won't have your room keys. And second, you will report to your mother and me everything you do. Also, you won't have your smartphone. I will give you an old phone that you can only call from," Richard paused for a moment. He then narrowed his eyes, as he was staring into her eyes, and said, "Do you understand?" Anna just nodded. Rita grinned. It was obvious enough for Anna to see her through the rearview mirror.

After arriving, Anna rushed to her bedroom. She threw herself on the bed and quickly texted Michael; knowing that any minute now, her father would take her phone. That being the case, she quickly reached for her second phone, which was hidden, and texted, "Good morning Michael, my phone will be taken from me. So, this is probably the last text you will receive from me. I will wait for you in the same café. PS. don't text me back."

As she was stashing the phone again, Richard marched in her room. He asked Anna to give him the key. Anna quickly hid her phone before calmly handing the key over. "And the spare key," dictated Richard. Anna reached for her desk drawer to get the key. As Richard was heading out, Anna reported, "I'm heading out to have breakfast."

"Where to?" inquired Richard.

"I don't know. I will try to find a good place for breakfast," responded Anna.

"All right, but don't be late."

Anna closed her door to wear her clothes. She went outside and drove to the café while hoping for Michael to read and comprehend her message.

DINNER

Michael received the message from Anna and prepared to go meet her. He packed his backpack and then went downstairs He told his parents that he was going to a café to have a cup of coffee. Michael wasted a lot of time trying to prevent Isabella from tagging along. He knew that she would ruin everything. Michael arrived at the café late. He found Anna sitting at the corner table. Michael took a deep breath then approached her. "Hey… Anna?" whispered Michael; his voice was clear enough for Anna to hear and turn around to face him.

Michael gently laid his back on his chair and then went to order. Anna patiently waited for Michael to finish ordering. When he returned to his chair, Anna started the conversation. "I went with my parents to see whether I was clean or not. But even after they knew I was clean, my father couldn't trust me anymore. He took my room key and wanted me to tell him everything I do. Also, he will soon take my phone. I mean, I'm eighteen for God's sake!"

Michael felt like this was the perfect time to start the plan.

He took his laptop out of his backpack and sat it on the table. He then asked Anna to come close so that she could see the screen. "As you have noticed, I have already started planning for the escape," whispered Michael, and then continued, "I have chosen three countries." On the screen three names were shown, Argentina, Iceland and Sweden. Both were silent, before Anna asked, "So, which country did you choose?"

"I haven't chosen any yet. But if we were to look at each one at a time, we can see that Argentina has nice weather and people. The fact that it can be unsafe sometimes and we don't know Spanish crossed it off the list. Moving on, we've got Iceland. The country is one of the safest countries in the world. Yet, the language is the issue here."

Michael stopped, then continued, "The last one which I believe is the best option, Sweden. It's true that we don't know the language, but English is widely spoken there. Plus, we might have better university options. Yes, I know that it's far away. But I believe it's worth the risk. So, what do you think?" Anna showed a puzzled face. She didn't know what to do. "Um, are these the only countries?" she inquired.

"Do you have another place in mind?" responded Michael. "Actually, I think that I do. What about Dubai?" suggested Anna. "Dubai you say? I've never visited it before. So, I don't know anything about the place," remarked Michael.

"Don't worry, I've traveled there with my family countless times. The place is safe, and there is a fair number of people who speak English," explained Anna.

"Is that so? Then I have no problem. We can go there. But, what about our future there?" asked Michael. He wanted to be sure that he could continue his study there. "Don't worry, the universities aren't the best in the world; yet they are the top in that region," explained Anna.

"Then it's settled; we are going to Dubai!" rejoiced Michael.

"Before we continue, let me tell you something," spoke Anna, "My family have this tradition, where they would go every summer to one of their summer houses. They have one in five countries, or so I remember. They will go the Monday night," she explained.

"Wait, that's the night of my graduation ceremony. But, if they will go, doesn't that mean you will have to go too?" inquired Michael.

"No, I won't go. I will try to persuade them to let me stay home. Even though it will be tough giving the fact that they suspect me of being an addict," answered Anna. She will have to find a reasonable reason to convince her parents.

"Fine, try your best to stay behind," said Michael. It was already noon when Michael realized he had to return home, so did Anna. They agreed to meet the next morning in the park.

ANNA RETURNED HOME, she went to her room. Anna still hadn't recovered enough energy, so she wanted to nap. She set the alarm to go off in two hours, and around lunchtime. After two hours, the alarm woke her up. She went down and took her tray back to her room. Her family was eating when she came. Neither Anna, nor her family talked to each other. They didn't even exchange looks. After finishing her lunch, Anna opened her door to leave the tray. The moment she closed her door, Anna heard a knock. It was Richard, with an old phone in his hand. "I found this phone, take it and give me yours," demanded Richard. Anna went to her desk to grab her phone. She then tried to take the sim card out of her phone, but Richard stopped her. "Oh no, you now have a new number." She handed her phone over and received her new phone; which wasn't "new."

While Anna was with Michael in the café, Richard called one of his friends and told him to bring a special phone. This phone was modified so that Richard could track all calls and text messages. After handing her the phone, Richard went back to his room, while Anna closed the door and started to play around with the phone. After a while, she noticed that a chip was installed inside the phone. She didn't know the reason behind it; yet, she had a few ideas.

Anna texted Michael using her second phone saying, "As expected, they took my phone. Delete the number associated with that phone. And keep in mind that I won't always be able to contact you using this phone. Most of the time, it will be hidden away from my parents. See you tomorrow."

Meanwhile in Richard and Rita's bedroom, the two were talking about their upcoming trip. "About our summer trip. Don't you think it's better to keep Anna home as a punishment?" suggested Rita. "Actually, I want her to attend rehab classes. That's why it would be a great idea to let her stay home. We can let the butler stay with her to watch her," remarked Richard. They both agreed on leaving Anna behind.

"What about her car? Did you install the GPS?" inquired Rita.

"No, not yet. I took them from a friend along the phone.

Tonight, when Anna sleeps; I will install it," explained Richard.

Anna was reading her new Manga book when she heard a knock on her door. As she reached for the door to open it, Richard was already opening it. "Anna, we have decided that you won't be coming with us on our summer trip. Instead, you will stay here for rehab. We will have the butler monitor you while we are gone," stated Richard; his voice was deep, which was unusual for him. On the other hand, Anna felt a huge relief. She didn't have to do the convincing; yet, her parents gave her what she wanted directly.

"What? The test showed that I was clean. Plus, I already told you I don't do drugs," Anna pretended to care.

"We've been over this. Anyway, starting next Monday, you will go to the rehab class. And our trip will be on the same day. You got that?" as Richard was talking, Anna saw Rita from behind grinning yet again. At this point, Anna was almost sure that Rita was behind this.

"Fine, fine, I got it," responded Anna. She wanted to play along, just to be less suspicious.

MICHAEL WAS in his room searching about Dubai. While the whole house was looking forward to meeting Taylor's family, Michael didn't really care. After all, he wouldn't marry her. Hours have passed, and it was time. The James family arrived. They rang the doorbell twice before the door was opened. "Good evening, please come in," said Lisa welcoming James and his family.

Both James and his family were seated in the dining room.

The butler served them, he offered them a glass of wine. Lisa then joined them as they were waiting for both Larry and Michael. Larry was already on his way down. He went to his son's room to make sure that Michael was well dressed. "Are you ready? Just act cool and don't ruin this dinner," ordered Larry. Michael just nodded absentmindedly.

Larry entered the dining room first and sat on his chair, and then Michael walked in. He tried to act cool and distributed his looks evenly on everyone seated; before taking a seat. But unfortunately for him, he was seated across Taylor's seat. He tried to look at her face for a moment, but quickly shifted his gaze once Taylor looked back at him.

"So, have you graduated yet Michael?" asked James. Michael looked deeply into James's eyes before saying, "The ceremony is next Monday."

"Is that so?" laughed James.

Michael was showing a serious face. But Larry looked him in the eyes. Larry's eyes were saying, "be less serious, and show a smile." Michael realized what Larry was trying to say and showed a fake smile across his face.

After almost seven minutes of talking, the food arrived. Three huge plates filled with salad were placed along the table. The cook then filled the plates of each guest except Michael. He wasn't hungry. In fact, he was full. While waiting for the main dish to come, Michael was scattering his looks all over the table. "Why don't you have some, honey?" asked Lisa. Michael thought of a suitable reason to convince her.

"I'm saving some space for the main dish," explained Michael.

Taylor was silent the whole time, she didn't say anything.

Lisa wanted to warm the water, so she inquired, "So Taylor, how is university going so far?"

"It's great. I'm doing fine," answered Taylor, with a calm voice.

The atmosphere was almost dead until the cook knocked on the door before entering. "Main dish is ready," he reported.

He sat the dishes; each guest had a plate for himself. The cook then collected the empty salad dished before exiting of the room. The dish was a filet mignon, served with mushroom sauce.

"Looking forward to next Tuesday. Right Sharlie?" stated James, with a mouth full of meat. "Yes, we sure do!" replied Sharlie.

"Speaking of which, have you written your guests list?" asked Lisa.

"As a matter of fact, we did. We also sent the invitations to our guests," explained Sharlie, and then asked, "What about you?"

"So did we! The wedding will be at your garden. Is that right?" remarked Lisa.

"That's right, I will make sure that Taylor will have the wedding of her dreams," added James.

After eating the dessert, which was fruit tart, both families continued chatting.

Taylor suddenly snapped and asked, "Where is the toilet?" Her eyes were locked on Michael. She was trying to tell him to come with her. As Lisa was telling Taylor the directions, Michael realized what Taylor wanted. "Take the first right, then—" Michael interrupted Lisa, and insisted, "I will show her the way."

"All right then," approved Lisa.

Both Taylor and Michael went past the door, and to the toilet. On the way, Michael took a left turn. They ended near the back exit of the house. "You wanted to talk?" asked Michael.

"Yes, I do," Taylor took a long breath then begged, "Please, I don't want to marry you. I have another one in mind; but my parents don't know about him. There is nothing wrong with you. It's just that I promised my friend." Michael felt like a huge load was lifted off his chest. "Actually, me neither; I don't want to get married to a woman older than me," explained Michael.

"Thanks, thank you very much. But, how will we convince our parents? They probably see benefit in the other family that's why they wanted us to get married," inquired Taylor.

"We won't convince them. After all, we both know they won't listen to us."

Michael paused for a moment, "Actually," he said, "we don't have much time. Do you know the park near my house?"

"Um… I think we passed by it on our way here," remarked Taylor.

"Great, meet me tomorrow morning there. I will tell you the details then."

"Ok, is ten good? Because I will have a class till nine thirty," inquired Taylor.

"Yeah, ten is great," answered Michael, as they were returning to the dining room. Taylor and Michael entered the room together.

"There you are. We are ready to leave," James said.

"Fine, then I'll go bring the car," remarked Taylor.

"We enjoyed our time here. And Lisa, the dinner was

delightful. Give the cook my regards," Sharlie stated. "I'm glad that you enjoy it. See you next Tuesday," added Lisa.

"See you soon, Larry. Keep up the good work!" beamed James.

"Will do!" responded Larry, with a smile.

Taylor's family returned, and Michael went to his room. Meanwhile, Larry was in his study room; he heard a knock on his door. "Come in," called Larry.

"Sorry, to interrupt you sir. But I believe I have something that might grab your attention," reported the butler.

"Speak," demanded Larry.

"I overheard Michael talking to Taylor alone. He said something about meeting her and not wanting to marry her. I'm not sure though."

Larry stood up and snarled, "Does Lisa know anything about it?"

"No sir, I only told you," explained the butler.

"Don't you say a thing in front of Lisa? And leave the rest to me," dictated Larry.

The butler nodded and then exited the room. "So, you wanna play with me Michael? Fine, I'll play with you," thought Larry while twisting his mustache.

TRUST

Richard made sure Anna was asleep before taking her spare car key from his closet. It was almost midnight when he went to the parking lot. Along with the GPS kit he got from a friend, Richard planted the GPS under the passenger seat and made sure it wouldn't fall. He also had another device that could listen to the conversation within the car. After completing his mission, Richard quickly retreated to his bedroom. Waiting there was his wife, Rita. She wanted to make sure that he installed the GPS in Anna's car. Meanwhile, Anna's car was left unlocked. As Richard forgot to lock it after he installed the GPS.

Anna woke up early, even before her alarm. She looked at her phone, which was on the table beside her; it was 8:00AM. Anna then took her second phone out of her stash. She found one unread message, and it was from Michael. He said that they will meet around 10AM.

"Now what to do? I have two hours till the meeting," wondered Anna. After giving it some thought, she decided to have breakfast at the café. It was the same café she often met Michael at. Anna dressed and then went down to the kitchen.

"I will have breakfast outside," Anna told the cook who was cooking breakfast.

"As you wish," replied the cook.

Anna went to her parked car and opened the door, "That's strange, I'm sure that I locked my car yesterday; unless..." thought Anna.

She then started the car and drove to the café. While she was on her way, she was thinking randomly about who could open the car. Or why the car was opened in the first place. It seems like the stuff inside the car was left untouched. And it was obvious that whoever unlocked the car had the keys.

"So, it's probably my parents, or the butler. And since nothing was stolen, it's safe to assume that it was my parents," the thoughts were swimming in Anna's head aimlessly.

She arrived at the café and ordered a breakfast meal consisting of a cup of coffee, a sandwich and a piece of chocolate. She sat down in her usual seat and ate her breakfast; meanwhile, Richard was wiping his face with a towel. He then realized that Anna wasn't in her room. Richard quickly opened his laptop and launched the GPS tracking software. On the map was Anna's car parked near a what seems to be a café. Richard grabbed his phone and called Anna's new phone.

Anna explained that she thought he was asleep; therefore, went to have breakfast without telling him. The only reason Richard called was to make sure the GPS was accurate, and it was. After finishing her breakfast, Anna stood up and went past the door. She looked at her smartphone, which she brought with her along the phone Richard gave her - there was still one-hour before the meeting. Anna then decided to head to the nearby park. She was about to start her car when she snapped, "Just in case, I'll walk to the park," she thought. Although Anna wasn't sure that her car was tracked, she just wanted to be on the safe side. Just in case the car was indeed tracked by someone.

After 15 minutes of walking, Anna arrived at the park. She sat near a pond. A flock of ducks was swimming freely; her eyes were locked to them. Anna watched as the ducks moved with no boundaries. She was in her own little world when Anna heard, "Yo, Anna." It was Michael; with what seemed to be another woman. Anna was showing a puzzled face as she has no clue about the identity of the woman. "Anna, this is Taylor. She is my fiancée, or so it should be," explained Michael.

Anna finally understood; she was somehow happy after hearing that the women had no real connection to Michael. Anna couldn't understand why, but she felt happy with Michael being "single." The only question that Anna had in her mind was "why she is here?"

"Nice to meet you, I'm Taylor," Taylor introduced herself to Anna.

"I'm Anna," She replied softly. Anna then stared at Michael in his eyes. She was waiting for an explanation.

"It's all right Anna," Michael remarked, then continued, "She already knows about the plan." Anna took a moment to process this new information. "I told her about my escape, since she really didn't want to marry me, anyway," explained Michael and then sat down between Anna and Taylor.

"It's not that I hate Michael or anything. I just have someone that I want to be with," remarked Taylor.

"So, Michael, what's the plan?" inquired Taylor.

Michael took a long breath while both girls were waiting for him eagerly. "Anna and I will escape that night before the wedding. We will go to Dubai; but we do have a problem, both our parents are keeping a close eye on us."

"My parents will be out of town, so my house will be all for me," Anna spoke and then stopped. She remembered something, "By the way, you should know this Michael; I came here walking and left my car at the café. Someone messed with my car last night. I made sure I locked it yesterday; yet, I found the door unlocked today." Michael thought for a moment before responding, "Just in case, for the next few days, only use your car for everyday stuff. Don't come to our meeting places riding that car," Anna was nodding while listening.

"Anyway, back to our main problem, we need to find a time when my parents lower their guard. I have already talked with my driver. But I didn't tell him the plan yet. Also—" Michael stopped and shifted his gaze to Taylor, "We might need you to help us, Taylor."

"I'm willing to do anything to prevent the wedding from happing," remarked Taylor.

"Great, you will act as a cover for our escape," remarked Michael, and then continued, "My mom is a double spy. She acted like she was against the whole marriage thing. But, later, I overheard her conversation with my dad. She has something to gain from this plan. Since my dad trusts her, I can use her to our advantage."

"Um, do you know what you will do once you are in Dubai?" inquired Taylor.

"We already got the money. So, we must find a place to live in and a university. Am I right Michael?" Anna responded.

"Yeah, something like that. Plus, I bet we can find a place to work a part-time job in," explained Michael.

"So, to put it simply, you will attend your graduation ceremony then escape the next week on Thursday, the night before the wedding; yet you want to do so without the notice of your parents. Is that correct?" inquired Taylor.

"Exactly," answered Michael, and added, "That's why we need to move after midnight, when everyone is sleeping. I will go with my driver to pick Anna, who will wait at the park. Then we will head to the airport. Meanwhile, Taylor will try to cover for us the next morning," Michael then stood up and said, "I have my laptop in Taylor's car. Taylor, can you give me the keys?"

"Um, sure, there you go," replied Taylor, as she was handing Michael the keys. Anna and Taylor were alone as Michael was jogging to the car.

"So, why are you against the wedding that much? I mean Michael is a nice guy," inquired Anna.

"It's not that I don't love him or anything. It's just that I already have a guy waiting for me. Plus, I believe the age difference is not fair for Michael; He deserves someone younger than me," Taylor explained. Both girls then sat still till Michael returned with his laptop.

"All right now, let's see what we have here," Michael said, while opening a flight search website. After entering all the information, Michael clicked on the 'search for flights' button. A list of flights showed on the screen. There were a lot of choices for Michael and Anna to choose from.

"How about this one?" Anna pointed at a flight. "The departure and arrival time seem better than the rest," she explained.

Taylor, who was sitting on the left side of Michael said, "I agree with Anna. This flight is the best option for you as you will fly for almost seventeen hours. Plus, this flight will only stop once; other flights will stop twice,"

"Quite the traveling expert!" remarked Anna.

"Well, I love to travel myself. I usually travel alone, so I built my experience based on my trips," explained Taylor, and then flicked her eyes back to Michael, "What do you think?" Michael took some time staring at the flight details. He then made his decision, "I believe this is the best option; as you both said."

"I'm gonna need your information, Anna," added Michael.

"I can send them via e-mail, I guess," replied Anna.

"Now we need to focus on the university. Also, Taylor, you can leave if you want. You don't need to waste your time any longer; I told you everything you need to know," requested Michael.

"Fine, if you say so," sighed Taylor. She stood up and faced both, "Good luck!"

Taylor left, and the two continued searching for a university. "So, Anna… what do you want to study? For me, I always wanted to be an engineer," asked Michael.

"Hmm… well my GPA isn't that great, so a business major will do fine.."

The three searched and settled on a university called 'UAM'. "I think this is the one. It accepts both engineering and business, so we should be fine. Plus, it's one of the top universities out there. Only the wealthy can afford it," remarked Michael.

"Well, if you say so… I guess we can enroll in it. But do you think we can meet all the requirements in time?" inquired Anna

"Don't worry, with my father as the district attorney, it will be easy," remarked Michael.

After settling on a university, Michael contacted the university to enroll in it. Anna looked at her phone's clock then snapped, "It's getting late. I told my parents I'm only having breakfast. I need to return now, or otherwise they will suspect something."

"All right then, I've already sent the request to the university. You need to send me your documents, so I can book the flight. I will find a good place for us to stay. Remember to act normally," remarked Michael.

Anna ran back to her car that was parked near the café. She quickly headed back home and silently entered her room. Anna then captured and sent Michael the required documents.

MICHAEL PACKED his stuff and called his driver. After Taylor and Anna left, Michael had no one to return home with. After almost fifteen minutes, his driver David had arrived. Michael was standing near the park's main entrance when he saw David approaching. Michael was reading a book he brought with him. He saw his house through the window then exclaimed, "Turn left David!"

"But sir, the house is the other way," David said, as he was turning left. Michael saw an empty alley and told David to stop.

"Is something wrong sir?" inquired David.

"Remember our last conversation?"

BIRTHDAY

David hesitated for a moment; his memory could not serve him as it used to.

"Oh yeah, I remember. It's that favor you asked the last day of school," he at last responded.

"Exactly," Michael replied and then stopped to take a deep breath. Michael then continued, "You see, David, I trust you the most."

David interrupted and said, "Well thanks, Sir. I appreciate those words." Michael smiled then resumed, "Anyway I want to escape this house."

David's blissful face turned into a serious face. Even Michael was surprised of this transform of emotions. But Michael did expect something like this to happen. "Michael are you aware of what you are saying?" David inquired, "I won't interfere with your decision; but, why? Why would someone living in this 'paradise' want to escape?" David continued.

His voice escalated. "It's not about how I am living. It's about what I had, and still am, paying for it. I lost my past for my parent's sake. No friends, no going out or having fun. It was all studying and attending meetings with my dad. And now? I'm about to throw away my dreams of being an engineer just to be a judge, like my father wanted. Also, in a few days, I will marry a woman I don't know and have no bond with her. I can continue if you want," Michael explained. A few tears found their way out of his otherwise dry eyes; Michael wiped them at once. Even after eighteen years of service, this was the first time David knew about this. He always thought Michael and Isabella were living the dream.

"I need your help. Please, you are the only one I can count on," requested Michael.

"As I said, I won't interfere with your decisions. Will you go alone? And what about the bride? Does she know anything?" David had a lot of questions to ask.

"Don't worry, I won't go alone. I had a friend called Anna; she will accompany me. Plus, I already talked to Taylor; she was against the wedding from the start. I just want you to drive us to the airport," explained Michael.

David thought about what he was putting himself in. He then inhaled and exhaled then said, "All right, Michael, I will help you. Even thought I might lose my job. As long as you are free to do what you want; I have nothing to lose."

"Thanks David, I appreciate it. I really do," rejoiced Michael.

"Now let us return home. I told Larry that I will only pick you from the park. He might start worrying that something happened," remarked David.

"You're right let's go," replied Michael.

Both entered the car, and headed back home. Waiting for them was Larry, who wasn't pleased with what he had heard yesterday. Michael opened the main door; with Larry standing on the other end. "Took you so long to return home from 'the park', won't you say so?" asked Larry suspiciously.

"Well, we got stuck in traffic," responded Michael.

"Traffic, huh? Anyway, get ready, we will go to have brunch in half an hour," remarked Larry.

"But I'm not—" Before Michael could finish his sentence, Larry interrupted him and said, "You MUST come today. It's a special lunch after all."

"Special lunch?" Michael thought.

"Do you mean mom's birthday? I thought we'll throw a huge party in our house like we always did," inquired Michael.

He just remembered that today was her birthday. "While we are at the restaurant, a group of people I hired will proceed with preparing the house for when we return."

Michael nodded and went past Larry; heading to his entertainment room to pick a book from the library. Michael chose a random book and started reading. "Michael, you in there?" said a familiar voice that Michael recognized immediately.

"Yes, come in." He stared at Isabella as she opened the door, holding a piece of paper.

"I made this for mom; sign here and write something sweet for her," demanded Isabella. Michael was just not in the mood. But he knew that no one could oppose Isabella; so he took the pen and wrote whatever came to his mind.

"Are we done here? If yes, please get out and close the door. I want to read alone," he insisted. Isabella quickly took the paper then retreated out of the room closing the door behind her. Not long afterwards, Michael was called by Larry to join them downstairs.

The family then went to have brunch in a nearby restaurant. The restaurant was packed. But, fortunately, Larry had already made a reservation beforehand.

"Can you just give me a second?" Larry told Lisa, who was heading towards her table.

"Where are you going? Is it work?" asked Lisa.

"Um, yes it's work. I'll be right back," hesitated Larry.

Larry exited the restaurant and dialed a number. "Hello? It's me. Are you ready? The home is all clear."

"Yeah, we got it. Do we start now?" Inquired the man on the other end of the call.

"Yes, go now, before we return home. And if anyone asks, tell them you are with the party organizers," answered Larry, then hung up and dialed another number. "The house is clear now; go and prepare for the party. You can use the butlers if you want," spoke Larry.

"All right. But we will need some time," said the party organizer.

"I'll give you two hours maximum. You need to be wrap things up be on your way by then. I will send you the cheque later today," explained Larry, before hanging up and returning to his family. Before arriving at his table, Larry went to a waitress and said, "I have already ordered when I reserved the table."

"Yes, Sir—the order is being prepared right now. We will bring the dishes according to how you specified," replied the waitress. "Good. Keep in mind that this is my wife's birthday, so don't mess things up," said Larry and returned to his table.

"Sorry for being late," apologized Larry.

At Michael's home, two groups were working. The first group was told to prepare for the party while the second group was assigned to plant the listening devices in Michael's bedroom. David was given the task of hanging the decorations along the stairs. While doing his job, David heard a noise coming from the second floor. Before going up to check, he counted the staff quickly, and they were all downstairs. He was pretty sure that they were the only people in the house. David snuck up the stairs and followed the source of the noise. It was coming from Michael's room. He peeked into the room while making sure they didn't notice him. He saw three men hiding stuff in the room. David couldn't see what they were hiding, yet he knew it had something to do with Michael's escape. "Did his parents know about the plan?" wondered David and then returned to his work.

After eating brunch, the family walked by the beach side. Once again, Larry called to check on the two groups after making sure both had finished their job. Larry returned with his family home. Isabella and Michael entered the house first to check on the guests, and to put the finishing touches. Larry waited with Lisa outside for the sign. And after seeing the sign, he opened the door while holding Lisa's hand with his other hand. Suddenly, lights switched on, and balloons were dropping from the ceiling. "Surprise! Happy Birthday!" exclaimed everyone.

The atmosphere was rich with smiles and laughter. But not everyone was enjoying it. Michael felt like he was wasting his time. He couldn't care less about a birthday. Lisa saw Michael sitting away from everyone. She at once approached him and asked, "Honey, what's wrong?"

"I don't feel well," replied Michael, while portraying a worried face.

"It looks like you helped a lot today. Go rest in your room," remarked Lisa.

"All right. And Happy Birthday Mom," Michael whispered back, with a faint smile. Michael managed to escape this boring event. He went to his room and locked the door. Michael's phone rang; David was calling. Michael reached for his phone and answered.

"Michael, are you home?" asked David.

"Um, yes I am," replied Michael.

"Can you meet me outside?"

"Is everything all right?"

"Just meet me outside."

"All right, I'm coming now," Michael ended the call. He snuck outside without Lisa noticing. She was too busy celebrating her birthday party.

"What's going on David?" asked Michael.

"I saw something that I believe you should know about," David took a breath before continuing, "while I was preparing for the party, I heard noises in your room. So, I tried to see who was in your room. I found strange men that weren't part of the team. I also saw them installing something, but I couldn't see what it was. I don't know what it was, but I believe that you need to be extra cautious."

"Is that so? Thanks for telling me David. I'll try to figure out what it is," said Michael and then snuck in back to his room.

Michael thought about what David had told him. He became quite curious about what was stashed in his room. Michael exited his room and went to check on his parents; they were still down. He then quickly returned to his room and locked the door before taking a good look at his surroundings. He was trying to see what had changed. As much as he wanted to find out what was hidden, Michael didn't want to cause extra noise. Just in case it was what he believed it was. After searching the surface places, Michael glanced at his small library. "Maybe, just maybe," he muttered. He shoved his hand behind the library and felt a strange thing. Michael slowly grabbed it to take a closer look at it.

"What's that?" wondered Michael as he was toying with what seems to be a small device. Suddenly the device's lower piece slid open. Michael found a small SIM card. It was at this moment that Michael realized what was going on. "A listening device, huh," he thought. Before brainstorming his next step, Michael returned the device to its place and searched for the rest. He believed that there could be other devices in the room. Michael gave up the search after finding a total of three listening devices scattered across the room.

"I don't know who's behind this; but I will play along…"

CEREMONY

FOUR DAYS LATER, IT WAS FINALLY THE BIG DAY FOR MICHAEL. He woke up unmotivated, mainly because today was his graduation ceremony. The fact that Larry will attend as the district attorney gave Michael no choice but to go along. He wiped his eyes and then checked his phone clock. Michael then quickly hopped out of bed and washed his face. During the past couple of days, he was collecting all sorts of documents for his escape. He also booked the flight and found a good hotel. Anna met with him to hand over any relevant documents. Now, Michael and Anna were waiting for their acceptance letter from the university. If they succeed in escaping, Michael believed that whether they got accepted or not wouldn't be a problem. They could always find other universities.

Michael ate breakfast alone since Larry was at work. And Lisa was still sleeping. They both decided to finish work early so that they could attend the ceremony. Michael then returned to his room. For the past few days, he had been thinking about the listening devices he found hidden in his room. Who was behind them, and what exactly was their motive? "Do my parents know anything about my escape?" wondered Michael. Just in case, Michael told Anna and Taylor about what he had found. Michael also stated that he would only contact them using the messaging app. Therefore, any information given by the phone will only be a mislead to whoever was listening through the device hidden in Michael's room.

Michael checked his clock one last time to make sure he was on schedule. He took a quick refreshing shower and put his suit on. The plan was for him to head to the location before his parents - who would arrive later? The graduation ceremony will take place in a football field. Michael's phone vibrated in his pocket. It was a text message, and the sender was Anna. Michael took his phone and read the message as he was preparing.

"So, today's the day! I just wanted to wish you luck. And as planned, we will meet tonight in the park. Right?" texted Anna.

Michael quickly replied with a thumbs up emoji as he was in a hurry. David was already waiting for him outside. Although the ceremony starts around one, the students had to be there by nine for rehearsals.

"It's finally the day, Michael," David spoke as he was driving to the stadium. He saw it all since Michael's first day at school. And now, after almost twelve years, it was all over.

"Yeah...," hesitated Michael. Deep inside, Michael knew that David was prouder of him than Larry. Or even Lisa, for that matter.

Michael arrived at the location stated in the invitation. The students had already started preparing. Someone approached Michael from behind and tapped his shoulder. "You're late Michael," Michael turned his face to realize it was Jimmy. It wasn't a surprise for Michael. Knowing Jimmy, Michael knew that he would try to find anything against him.

"Sorry for being late, again," spoke Michael with pride in his voice. Jimmy's face was certainly showing rage and anger. Jimmy tried to control himself and demanded, "Come on, go help your friends prepare."

"Friends? Hmpf, don't make me laugh," muttered Michael as he was passing Jimmy.

"What did you just say?" snapped Jimmy. He was triggered even though he didn't hear what Michael had said. Michael ignored Jimmy and made his way to the rest of his "friends." After a boring three and a half hours, parents started to enter, and the preparations were over. While Michael didn't exactly do much, he was frustrated by how his time was being wasted. The students were seated in the seats assigned to them earlier. The seated were divided into a block for students, a line or two for teachers, and the rest were guest seats.

Unfortunately for Michael, his seat was the last in the students' row, which meant that the next seat beside him was his jealous teacher's seat. Michael didn't realize that until he saw Jimmy approaching him and sitting right next to him. Michael was in his little world when he heard the clapping; Larry had arrived. Larry waved at the guests as he walked toward his seat at the front. Before sitting, he gave Michael an expressionless look. Michael couldn't understand the deep meaning behind it. The school president stood up the stage and started his speech. There was great applause when he sat down. Soon afterwards, Larry stood up and walked to the stage. He spoke for a solid 15 minutes till he noticed the guests getting bored. He then thanked them one last time and returned to his seat.

The vice president cleared his throat and started saying the student's names. Larry and the school principal stood up to hand certificates. Michael was on the honorary list; he was fourth. Even though Michael was proud of his achievement, Larry wasn't that proud. He wanted his only son to be at the top of that list. Michael's name was finally announced.

He stood up, gave Jimmy the 'I'm better than you' look, then walked to the stage. He shook hands with Larry. Both exchanged looks that had a lot to say. Michael then walked to the school president, who was holding the certificate. Michael took the certificate and stood between him and Larry waiting for the photographer to click the shutter button. Michael glanced at David sitting with the guests; he saw David shedding some tears. He couldn't be blamed, not after serving Michael since his birth.

Michael was forced to sit through the rest of the ceremony. After the ceremony was over, people started to gather for a small outdoor buffet. Michael couldn't care less about the food. He immediately started looking around for David.

"David, we're going back," waved Michael as he approached him. As for David, he just filled his plate and was ready to enjoy his food. He quickly took a few bites then hurried to the car. Larry saw Michael leaving, but he was busy talking with the school principal. Before entering the car, Michael took one last look around him.

"All right let's go," ordered Michael, and David nodded.

Michael arrived and was welcomed by his butler, who

opened the door for him. "Congratulations, Michael," said the butler.

"Thanks."

In his room, Michael switched on his computer to check on the progress of the plan. Michael heard a buzzing from his pocket; it was a text message. "Michael, where are you? Did you return early?" texted Lisa.

"Yes, I got bored and returned home," replied Michael.

Michael checked his e-mail and found a new mail from UAM:

"Dear Mr. Michael,

I am pleased to inform you that you have been admitted to the bachelor's degree program in Engineering for the 2018/2019 academic year beginning September 2018.

We are proud to have you as one of our students. Looking forward to meeting you soon.

Yours truly,

Vince Anders, PhD

Graduate Advisor."

Before celebrating, Michael quickly grabbed his phone and texted Anna. "Did you receive the acceptance letter?" Anna replied almost immediately, "Yes I got one. So, now what? What's next?"

"Next, huh?" thought Michael. "We still have some time before the escape. I guess we should slow down a bit; no need to rush the plan," he then texted.

"I see. But what about Taylor? I still don't trust her," replied Anna with a question. "Don't worry, I don't think she will expose our plan. After all, she is against the wedding," explained Michael.

Michael switched off the lights, and slowly inserted

himself into his bed for a quick energizing nap.

ANNA WAS in her room reading. While she had headphones over her ears, she could still hear her parents packing for the vacation. Anna didn't really care about the trip. After all, soon she was going to go on a trip of her own. "Anna, come out for a sec," called Richard.

Anna walked to the door, and replied without opening the door, "Is it important?"

"Just open the damn door!" ordered Rita; and Anna opened the door.

"As you already know, your mom and I will go to our summer house. You, on the other hand, will stay here and attend rehab," stated Richard.

"As you wish," replied Anna with a light smile.

"Come on honey, we're getting late," remarked Rita.

While both were walking, Richard stopped and turned his head towards Anna, "Take care of yourself." Anna nodded with her infamous stoneface expression. She then went downstairs to check who would monitor her. Anna took a peek while sitting on the steps. "Urgh, it's him," she muttered.

She had a bad past experience with him. That butler, George, was assigned to accompany Anna to school; he'd defend her against the bullies. They would avoid Anna while she was with him and bully her again in class. Anna returned to her room. She checked her clock. It was around 10PM. Of all possible hours her rehab class starts around 9AM. Anna thought she would watch a few episodes before going to sleep. Obviously, these 'few episodes' led to a late night as usual. Anna went to bed at 1AM, way past her bedtime.

"Anna, wake up. It's almost time," called George from the other side of the door. Anna slowly opened her eyes; the room was a mess. Food on the floor, and the lights were still on. "Just give me a sec," she called back, sweeping the food off the bedsheets.

Anna quickly grabbed the nearest dress and wore it. George must drive her to and from rehab. It was one of the many rules Richard imposed. He also asked George to stay outside the building where the class would be held.

"I'll be waiting in the car," remarked George.

Before exiting her room, Anna texted Michael: "I'm now heading to rehab. A butler will drive me and wait for me outside."

The two arrived at the rehab center after a ten-minute ride. "All right, off you go. I'll be waiting here in the car."

Anna arrived fifteen minutes early but still walked into the classroom. Just like every other rehab class, the chairs were forming a circle. Anna chose the furthest seat from the counselor. And as she was taking it all in, the door opened at once. A young boy entered. He was almost the same age as her. Anna opened her closed eyes and gasped the moment her eyes met him.

"Lucas?" she snapped.

"Yo, what's up, Anna," smiled Lucas, "Funny seeing you here; and here I thought you were that 'pure' Anna I once knew."

"Don't get the wrong idea. I was falsely accused." Explained Anna then added, "Never mind that, what about you? Did the breakup hurt you so bad that you started drinking?"

"Are you kidding me? I'm over this stupid relationship. Moreover, it was my mistake dating a weeboo like you. Also, it doesn't matter whether you were falsely accused or not, you are here now. And it will be a dark spot in your life," Lucas fired everything he was hiding since the breakup. They had been dating since their high school freshman year. After they became seniors, Lucas turned into one of the "cool" guys. Anna couldn't handle his actions any longer. She stormed into a room where Lucas used to hang with his buddies and broke up with him. In front of everyone.

Both stopped talking and waited patiently as the rest of the class started to enter the room. George waited for almost an hour till Anna left the building eventually. "So, how was the first session?" he inquired, as she was closing the car's door forcefully.

"Just drive!" ordered Anna with a cold face.

"Just so that you know, I believe that you are clean. After all, I can't imagine that the little Anna I know would do such things," remarked George. He then added, "I'll always be on your side."

"Thanks, I really do appreciate it," stated Anna as she was gazing out of the window.

"Um, hello?" Answered Rita.

"Good afternoon, ma'am. It's Lucas, your daughter's ex," spoke back Lucas.

"Yeah, I know who you are. Anyway, tell me about today," demanded Rita. "I did as you asked and joined the rehab. Looks like she's still mad," explained Lucas

I see, keep an eye on her," ordered Rita before hanging up.

Before heading for their annual vacation, Rita had reached for Lucas and asked him to keep an eye on Anna. While Lucas's parents weren't as wealthy as Anna's, Richard wanted him to be his son-in-law. He believed that his popularity at school and his personality would open doors for him in the future. Meanwhile, Anna arrived home and went straight to her room. She wasn't moved at all by seeing Lucas, or so she thought.

LUCAS

Anna woke up early, unlike every other morning. Mostly because she went to bed early the night before. While in bed, Anna kept thinking about her conversation with Lucas the other day. Engaging with her past, Anna lost track of time. Anna thought that since she had woken up early, she could probably have breakfast or something. But now, time ran out of her hand. She only had 5 minutes to prepare since George was already waiting in the car. Anna splashed some water on her face and dressed up.

"Sorry for being late," apologized Anna.

"No problem," replied George.

Anna barely made it on time, and the class was full. Unfortunately for Anna, the only seat left was the one next to Lucas. He waved at Anna and pointed at the chair near him. Anna sighed and walked to the chair.

"All right then, let's start today's session," remarked the instructor.

. . .

After two boring hours, the session was over. This time, it was longer, and she was seated next to Lucas.

"Anna, wait," called Lucas as Anna was about to leave the room. She slowly turned her head in Lucas's direction and sighed, "What? I'm kinda busy."

"I just want to tell you something," explained Lucas.

Anna sighed for the second time that morning. She returned and sat down. Lucas closed the class door and sat on the opposing seat. "Look, Anna. I just want to apologize for what happened yesterday. And no, I don't do drugs. I just came here because I heard that you registered here," explained Lucas.

Anna closed her eyes for a moment then opened them slowly, "I'm not sure how to explain this to you. But I love my current lifestyle and have no intention of changing it. While you might think that it's your mistake, let me clearly say that it's no one's mistake," Anna took a long breath afterwards.

"I see... It's just that since the breakup, I had no idea of what to do with my life. After graduation, all my friends scattered as if we were never together once," remarked Lucas then continued, "The way I see it; you found a new boyfriend. Am I right?"

"Huh? Are you crazy? I told you I'm done with relationships," snapped Anna. "I—" Anna's phone rang. She glanced at the caller ID and immediately stood up. "Sorry, my driver is waiting."

"I won't give up, you know!" yelled Lucas before Anna closed the door behind her.

Anna went to George who was waiting for her. On the other hand, Lucas grabbed his phone and started texting: "Good morning ma'am, I just spoke with Anna. Apparently, she's hiding something, a secret boyfriend for example. I'll try again tomorrow."

On her way home, Anna texted: "Michael, we need to meet; text me back."

MICHAEL WAS EATING a late breakfast when his phone vibrated in his right pocket. "Great, I also need to finalize the plan with you and David. When are you free?" he texted.

As usual, Michael got a response almost immediately. "I'm now with my driver. I can tell him to drop me near the park, and I'll walk to the café," texted Anna.

"All right try to act normal. I'll be there in ten." After finishing his meal, Michael called David and told him to bring the car. Michael went to his room to grab the documents he needed and slid them in his laptop bag.

"Where are you going this early?" inquired Isabella.

"Urgh. First, its almost noon. Second, I'm going to the cafe," explained Michael, not that he had to justify his daily itinerary.

"I want to go with you!" ordered Isabella.

"No. Don't think that I'll obey everything you say like mom and dad," Michael gave Isabella a dark stare then left.

"Fine, you wanna do it this way. Let's do it," thought Isabella showing her childish evil smile.

"Where to?" asked David.

"We're going to meet Anna to add the final touches to the plan. Go to that same cafe I often frequent."

"Understood…"

Michael arrived sooner than he had expected. He ordered

his usual coffee and sat in his usual spot. David, on the other hand, didn't order anything. He just sat in patience and waited for Anna. Michael spread his stuff on the table and opened his laptop.

"Well you're late. Where exactly did your driver drop you?" inquired Michael. Anna sat down then explained, "Not far away, but I had to distract him before I could come inside."

"I see, now let's start planning," said Michael.

"First, I need to clarify something," Anna said, "The reason I asked you to meet me here was because I met someone at rehab." Michael and David remained silent.

"My ex—"

"Your what?" snapped Michael.

"We were dating back in high school. But after he got cocky, I left him," explained Anna.

"I see, and now he attends the same class as you?"

"Yes, I'm not sure whether it's a coincidence or a planned move," Anna then inquired, "Anyways, how is the plan going? Any new updates?" David and Anna grabbed their chairs and moved them to each side of Michael's chair. This way, both could see what was going on.

"So far, we both graduated, got accepted at the same university, and bought a flight ticket. Last time we met, we booked a hotel. And since we won't need a visa, I think we are ready to go," explained Michael then continued, "Moving on, now we got the matter of actually escaping from our houses. With my parents staying up late, we have no choice but to escape after midnight. The flight will depart around 3AM, so we will have enough time."

"I agree with Michael. And I can wait in a place where the

surveillance cameras can't reach us. We then pick Anna from the park," remarked David.

"Anna, any objections?" asked Michael.

"None."

"All right then—"

"But what about Taylor?" Anna interrupted upon recalling Taylor's involvement with the plan.

"Oh yeah, Taylor will be our 'shield'. She will cover for us the next morning," answered Michael then turned his face towards David, "And David, you need to find an excuse for when my parents ask you."

"Don't worry, I'll figure something out," explained David.

"Now, the most important—" Michael's phone rang; it was Larry. "Sorry, I gotta take this," apologized Michael and left his seat.

"Michael, where are you now?" asked Larry.

"I'm currently sipping a cup of coffee…"

"And why didn't you bring your sister with you."

"I just needed some quality time alone."

"You know it doesn't work this way. Return home and pick up your sister," demanded Larry.

"But I just finished my coffee."

"So what? All I want you to do is to drive Isabella to that very cafe." ordered Larry before hanging up the call. Michael returned to his table with a disappointed face.

"Sorry Anna, I have to return. Come on David," sighed Michael.

"Something happened?" inquired Anna.

"Well, my sister wants me to drive her to a cafe. She got jealous, or rather clingy." explained Michael.

"Too bad. Well I guess we have to postpone our meeting for another time," remarked Anna.

"Will you be all right? You have no one to take you back home," asked Michael.

"Don't worry, I'll call my driver to pick me," answered Anna.

Michael and David went on their way while Anna was waiting for George.

"ANNA, I'M OUTSIDE," spoke George.

"Well that was fast."

"Yeah, I was driving near the café when you called," he explained.

Anna went outside and found the car parked near the entrance. "How did you manage to find a parking spot when the lot was full, and no one left the cafe?" inquired Anna.

"To be honest with you, I never left the parking spot. And yes, I saw almost everything. Who was he?" Anna's heart pounded in fear. She gathered her breath then calmly said, "I don't have to tell you."

"Please Anna, you know I care about you. I don't want you to fall into these traps at this age," explained George.

"Don't worry, it's not what you think it is. I don't intend to get into a relationship with anyone," Anna was trying to avoid spoiling everything.

After almost five minutes, the two reached the villa. As Anna was leaving, George stopped her for a moment, "Wait, Anna. Let me tell you one last thing. No matter what you do, I won't interfere with it. I assure you that nothing will reach your parent's ears."

"Thanks, George," smiled Anna.

She then returned to her little cave where she would enjoy her TV shows and Manga. Anna's phone rang at a time where she wouldn't expect any calls. To make things worse, it was an unknown number. A number she couldn't recognize no matter how hard she read it. Anna took a long breath and answered.

"Um, hello," spoke Anna.

"Hey, Anna. How are you?"

"Lucas!" Anna muttered as her heart pounded. Yet, this time, the blood rushed throughout her now tingling body.

"Helloo!" Lucas was confirming whether he'd got the right number or not.

"How did you get my number?" asked Anna with fear in her tone.

"It doesn't matter now. Though what does matter is that I'm standing by your door step outside. Come on open the door, let's chat!" Lucas gave Anna no other choice. She hung up, and looked through her window, which was covered by a shade. And there he was, waiting outside of her house. Anna couldn't prioritize these shocks.

"How does he know my number? Why is he at my doorstep? And most importantly why is he still trying to get me back?" wondered Anna as she was walking down the stairs.

"George," called Anna with a slightly low voice.

"Yes, Anna," replied George as he was rushing to her.

"I have a problem. On the other side of the door is my ex

waiting. He's in the same rehab class as me. And now, he is stalking me. He even managed to get my phone number," explained Anna.

"Got it. Just return to your room and I'll deal with this pest…" George waited for Anna to go up before opening the door.

"Took you long enough—" as Lucas uttered those words, he took notice of a huge body pulling the door open. A well-built physique wearing a dark suit stood between him and the door.

"How can I help you?" asked George.

"Yeah, I'm here to talk with Anna," replied Lucas. His eyes were fixed at the body of muscles.

"Too bad, she's not home," explained George.

"Well that's strange, I swear I saw her window's shade moving just now," doubted Lucas.

"Listen buddy, I said she's not home. Are we gonna have any problems?" George's voice deepened a bit. Lucas started to realize that his safety was more important than the mission he was assigned by Rita.

"N-no. We're good. Tell her when she returns that I said 'hi'," immediately afterwards, Lucas sprinted to his car and fled.

George waited to make sure Lucas was gone for sure, and then went back inside. "You're still here?" asked George.

"Yeah, I thought he might see me if I went to my room," explained Anna.

"Anyway, don't worry. He won't be bothering you anymore," George smiled his usual smile.

"Thanks George. I'm glad that he won't buzz here again," remarked Anna.

"Time is ticking. Let's hope we can pull this off," thought Anna as she was heading to her room. She knows the risk of escaping from her house only too well. Yet, she decided to have complete faith in Michael.

ENCOUNTER

WITH ALMOST SEVEN DAYS LEFT, MICHAEL BEGAN TO experience anxiety, more so than usual. He knew that things wouldn't go as smoothly as he planned. Yet, he was trying his best to lower the risk of him getting caught. Lisa was having a client in her room, and Larry went to the job he was proud of. Michael was wondering what to do with his morning. He then decided on continuing his meeting with Anna. But, this time, they would meet in the rehab center. Michael packed his stuff and left without making any noise. He didn't want Lisa to notice him exiting the house.

"It's almost time," thought Michael as he was driving to the rehab center. He waited outside for almost ten minutes before people started to leave.

"Anna!" waved Michael from his car. Anna realized it was Michael and rushed to his car. "Quick, drive before Lucas sees us," ordered Anna. Michael drove away at once. Hiding behind the main entrance was Lucas; he saw everything. Lucas waited till Michael's car disappeared before sneaking out of his hiding spot.

"Hello," called Lucas.

"Lucas? Why are you calling me at this hour?" asked Rita with a yawn.

"I thought you might be interested in hearing this," explained Lucas.

"What do you have? Make it quick, I'm busy."

"I just saw Anna entering a stranger's car. Judging from her face, she knows him."

"Is that all? Did she do anything after getting in the car?"

"Can't be so sure. The guy drove as soon as she closed the door," explained Lucas.

"All right wait here till she returns. After all, her driver, George, is waiting for her." Lucas hung up the call. "This is more than what I'm getting paid for," he sighed.

After driving away from the center, Michael stopped the car, "I think we will be all right here." Anna looked outside the widows just to make sure she was in the clear.

"Remember my ex that I told you about?" asked Anna.

"Yeah, what about him?"

"He started stalking me. Not only does he know that I was going to rehab; he even knew my phone number. Yesterday, he was standing at my doorstep. Thankfully, George, my butler, took care of him. But knowing him, I don't think Lucas will stop there. I bet he was spying on me the moment I got out of the building,"

"Is that so? Question is, who told him about your private life?"

"I don't know. Most importantly, why are you here?" inquired Anna.

"I thought we could continue our meeting. But apparently, you had bigger stuff to handle," explained Michael, and then continued, "I'll make it quick. First, I will wait for everyone to sleep. Then David and I will pick you from the park where you'll be waiting. Finally, David will drop us at the airport. Now what comes afterwards is the tricky part. We need to make sure they can't trace us."

"Since our parents are rivals, I don't think they will simply accept the fact that we escaped together," remarked Anna.

"I guess you are right," Michael then stopped talking and closed his eyes. "Um, are you, all right?" asked Anna.

"Yeah, I was just thinking about this Lucas. Did someone send him to spy on you? Or was he just stalking?"

Anna checked her clock then exclaimed, "I forgot George. He was supposed to drive me home."

"No problem, I can drive you home. Since we are already on the way. You can tell him to head back."

"All right, if you say so…"

ANNA CALLED George and explained that her friend was taking her home. Meanwhile, Lucas was waiting for Anna near George's car. Suddenly, the car moved without Anna.

"Where is he going?" he wondered from his hiding spot. He then at once texted Rita, before following George.

"Wait a minute, isn't this Anna's house?" thought Lucas as he parked within distance.

Luckily, Michael was near the house when he was talking to Anna. Therefore, he was able to arrive before George.

"Why, isn't Anna with her driver? Unless she didn't return home…"

"Anna, you in there?" asked George.

"Yes, I'm in my room."

"Anyway, who drove you back home," inquired George.

"A friend; I found her by coincidence," explained Anna.

"Is that so?" George got a call, and it was from Rita. "I heard that Anna didn't return with you today. Is that true?" asked Rita.

"Yes, she said it was her friend," explained George.

"Her friend?" asked Rita.

"Um, yeah…"

"Lucas said it was a guy, not a girl. What's going on?" thought Rita then remarked, "Did you see who she was?" asked Rita.

"No, I was in my car the whole time," explained George.

"All right, if you encounter her tell me immediately," ordered Rita.

As for Anna, she knows that a week is barely enough to prepare for an escape. She checked online for her bank account. "Yeah, that will do just fine," she assured herself.

Anna was saving for a while now; her only concern was whether to tell George or not. She felt that he deserved to know; yet, he might expose the plan to her parents. As Anna was confronting her dilemma, her phone rang. "Hello, Dad?" She answered.

"How are you doing?" inquired Richard.

"I'm fine, I guess," replied Anna.

"How was the rehab class?" asked Richard.

"Everyone is wondering why a clean person would attend rehab," Anna was trying to make a point.

"Don't listen to them. We both know why you are here," explained Richard then continued, "Anyway, stay safe and we will see you soon." Anna's heart pounded yet again. She calmed herself, then asked, "How soon?"

"This Friday, an old friend of mine invited me to attend his son's wedding," explained Richard.

"By any chance, were you talking about Larry? The district attorney?" inquired Anna. Her heartbeats were still inconsistent.

"Indeed, how did you know that?" answered Richard.

"Isn't he you rival?" remarked Anna.

"Yeah, so what—Well, time's up. Your mom is calling me. See you on Friday," Richard ended the call. Anna quickly texted Michael: "We have a problem; my parents are coming to your wedding."

"What?" replied Michael.

"Think about it, both parents will be together when they realize that neither the groom nor their daughter is here," texted Anna.

"Don't worry, we will be long gone by then. Try to empty your mind and don't get all stressed up. We still have a week to figure out everything," texted Michael, fidgeting his left hand.

THE WEEK FLEW by at an alarming rate, even for Michael. It was finally the day; the day Michael had prepared for since the last week of school. Michael woke up refreshed, yet a tad anxious. He tried his best to hide this little secret from his parents, unlike Anna who had a whole mansion to herself. After splashing drops of water on his face, Michael was fully awake. He went to check on his parents; he knew that Larry will go to work early, and Lisa promised to take Isabella shopping. Having that confirmed, Michael now had a few hours to enjoy alone. After eating breakfast, Michael went to his room to finish packing his bags. Although he started packing a while back, stuff like a toothbrush and deodorant had to be packed on the trip's day.

Since last week, Michael was meeting regularly with Anna in the rehab center. He joined as an addict just to get close to her and Lucas. After Lucas began suspecting him, Michael started to implant his message in his talking; and Anna would understand the message and reply back as she was speaking to the rest of the class. Everytime Michael spoke to the group, Lucas became more suspicious.

Finally, one day, he was at his limit. Lucas waited for Anna to exit the class then closed the door behind him. Only Michael and Lucas were left. Anna was supposed to meet Michael by his car. She told George to return home early.

"Hey, I gotta tell you. I'm impressed by your past, and how you are fighting your addiction. Yet, I can't help but notice that you don't have any physical effects. From the way you explained it; you should have at least red eyes. I mean, you don't even look pale," attacked Lucas, showing all his cards.

Meanwhile, Michael was sitting in his place with his eyes closed. After Lucas stopped talking, Michael opened his eyes slowly. "Splendid, you got a good eye; especially for an addict. I also did my own 'observation'. I even took it a step further than you. You see, I looked at your files. And I'm amazed by how they let you in here. 'Sleeping aids' really? Couldn't you find any other excuse to come here?" Lucas started to sweat. Michael continued, "Unless, the reason for you to come was something other than 'curing' this addiction. Stalking for example? Or perhaps wasting free time?" Lucas lost his cool and interrupted Michael, "I know why you are here."

Michael sensed the fear and anxiety in Lucas's voice, "Hmm, you think so?" Michael was trying to get Lucas to lose his composure. "I heard it with my own ears, Michael. I know you are here t—" Before Lucas got a chance to complete his deduction, the door opened.

"Anna!" both he and Michael snapped.

"What are you doing here?" asked Lucas.

"I forgot something," answered Anna then asked, "What about you guys? Staying together in a closed room alone. I can only think about—"

"It's not what you think!" yelled Lucas.

Anna took the pen she left on purpose and then gave Michael a look; Michael nodded slowly. "Look, Lucas? I have no idea what you want from me. All I know is that I'm a busy man. So, if you don't mind, I gotta go. See you soon though," explained Michael.

"Oh yes, you are a busy man indeed," replied Lucas with a serious tone. "You can't run away forever,"

"Try me," challenged Michael before leaving the room.

"Hello ma'am, it's me again. I think I have a guess on that 'friend' of Anna. His name is Michael. And I'm gonna prove it," texted Lucas.

"All right good job. Now leave the rest of the work to me. No need for you to continue. I'll send you the money we agreed on," replied Rita.

"No, I want to continue. I hate that guy, and I want to confirm that he was the one who stole my Anna!" texted Lucas.

"All right, but I'm not paying you a penny extra."

"Yeah, whatever…"

"You challenged me Michael; and I accept your challenge," muttered Lucas.

"What was that about?" inquired Anna; Michael was walking after her, as she anxiously walked back to his car.

"Lucas's onto us… I tried to play with him, but then you walked in." explained Michael.

"Be careful, it's finally the day. You don't wanna mess things up on the last day," remarked Anna.

"Yeah, you're right," replied Michael.

"More importantly," added Anna, "I'm still debating whether to tell George about our escape."

"He still doesn't know? I thought you told him."

"Well, I don't really trust that he will be quiet about it," explained Anna.

"Tell you what, why don't we meet him together? I can explain the situation to him. What do you say?" offered Michael.

"Hmm… But are you sure it'll work? I mean it's risky," noted Anna.

"All I can say is that it's a fifty-fifty chance. Either we win or lose it all. But he's your butler, so you should know him better than I would," explained Michael.

Anna gave it a long thought, before finally deciding, "All right, let's do it. But, when and where do you want us to meet?" inquired Anna.

"How about the park? After all, he won't be able to react in public," explained Michael.

"Fine, first I want to rest for an hour or so. Then, we will meet in the park around noon," remarked Anna.

"Fine by me," noted Michael, heading back to Anna's mansion.

"George," called Anna.

"Yes, did you want something?" inquired George.

"We need to talk."

"Sure, what's on your mind?"

"I know this might sound weird to you. But I want you to meet with me and my friend," explained Anna.

"Um... sure. Is she the one who started to drop you home?" asked George.

"Yeah, we will meet around noon in a nearby park. You'll drive," remarked Anna.

"All right, if you say so. I'll wait in the car by eleven thirty," George quickly returned to the kitchen, as his meal was almost ready. And since the cook traveled on his yearly vacation, George had to cook for him and Anna.

Meanwhile, Anna went to her room. After switching off the lights, she attempted to rest for an hour or so; as to be fully awake for the big escape. After a fulfilling nap, Anna woke up at the sound of her alarm. She quickly dressed and went for George who was waiting outside.

"All right, let's go," commanded Anna as she entered the car. She also sent a message to Michael telling him that she was on her way.

"Ma'am, Anna just left house with the driver. I'll follow them and see where they're headed," texted Lucas.

FAREWELL

"Where exactly is that park?" inquired George.

"Turn right then continue straight," explained Anna. According to his text, Michael had already arrived at the park.

"There, that park," pointed Anna. George dropped Anna near the entrance and went to find a place to park the car.

She strolled to the usual place and found Michael reading a book. "What you are reading?" asked Anna, as she approached him from behind.

"Oh, never mind that. More importantly, where is George?"

He still doesn't trust her. For him, she was a 'pathetic something' he will need to rescue. Unlike Anna, who had apparently fallen for him.

"George is just parking the car," explained Anna.

"So, what exactly will we tell George? How much does he need to know?" continued Anna.

"Enough for him to wake up the next morning and not be scared by the fact that you're not home," explained Michael.

As both were discussing, Lucas was hiding behind a tree.

He was far enough to be hidden; yet, close enough to hear what was going on. As Lucas was trying to get as much information as he could, he felt a tap on his back. Lucas quickly turned his back; it was George.

"Are you lost?" asked George.

"Um, no… I was just resting," replied Lucas hesitantly.

"I completely forgot about him. I thought he was just dropping Anna off," thought Lucas.

"I-I'll be on my way," hesitated Lucas.

"Oh, George we are here," waved Anna.

George and Michael kept their eyes fixed on each other. "George, this is Michael, a friend," explained Anna then continued, "Michael, this is George, my butler."

"Nice to meet you," said both Michael and George respectively.

"Strange," remarked George, "I can't seem to remember seeing Michael at your school. Not to mention, he is not a 'she', unlike what you had told me."

"Um, that's because he is from another school. And I had to cover up his gender for the plan to move smoothly; sorry," explained Anna.

"What? Since when do you know each other? And don't tell me you two are dating?" George snapped.

Before continuing his anger phase, Anna stopped him, "Calm down, George."

"Allow me to explain," insisted Michael. George calmed down and then sat dawn to listen. "First of all, we met almost a month ago. Moving on, no, we are not dating or anything," Michael looked at Anna, as nodded in agreement; deep inside she was a kind of disappointed. She was hoping for a better answer.

"So, that's basically it," remarked Anna.

"Then, why are you going out with her?" inquired George.

"That's why we brought you. To discuss this matter," noted Michael.

George's face became serious as he was about to hear the truth. "It all started that night…"

MICHAEL EXPLAINED EVERYTHING. From his first meeting with Anna, till today. George's face turned pale. He turned his face to Anna.

"Is that true? What he just said, is it true?" inquired George. "Yes," hesitated Anna.

"I just can't process this. Why would the daughter of a wealthy family want to escape with a guy? It just doesn't add up."

"It doesn't have to. Also, when you think about it, it's very simple. Our families betrayed us both. For me, I was controlled like a puppet for the last 18 years. And I don't know a lot about Anna; but her parents treated her almost similarly," remarked Michael.

"You know nothing about Anna. She—"

Anna interrupted George and explained, "Actually, you are the one who doesn't know a thing. You don't even know that I was falsely accused of drug possessing. You just heard the modified story, which my parents told you. Also, I'm pretty sure you don't know how they treated me when you were not there."

George lowered his face, "But still, you can't just escape…"

"Actually, I can. And I will—tonight," replied Anna.

"Tonight?" snapped George.

"Don't worry, we're well prepared," assured Michael.

"Where are you going?" asked George.

"Du—"

"I'm sorry, but we can't tell you now," Michael interrupted Anna before she could spoil the plan.

"Listen, I'm running out of time. I need to be home by now. We just wanted to inform you about our intentions. Any other information won't do you any good at this point."

Michael was about to stand when George grabbed his hand, "Wait! Just promise me this one thing," George fixed his eyes on Michael. "I'm trusting you with Anna. Please, keep an eye on her. She is the only thing I have left in this life," remarked George, as he was tearing.

"You are a good man George. I bet Anna's parents won't say what you just said. I promise, I will keep her safe," assured Michael, and Anna's heart pounded.

Michael called David, who was waiting in the parking lot. They both returned home just before Lisa's arrival. It was a close call.

"Michael, come downstairs," called Lisa. Michael sighed, then walked to where Lisa was, "Yes, Mom?"

"Ready for tomorrow? Are you missing anything?" inquired Lisa.

"No mom, I'm all ready!" replied Michael with a smile. He knew that since Lisa was a double spy, he would need to play it cool in front of her.

"Great, now go to the supermarket; I forgot to buy some stuff," remarked Lisa.

"Um, can't a butler go instead?" inquired Michael.

"They're busy with the preparations. So, you need to go, and I'll text you the list," demanded Lisa.

Michael drove to the supermarket. He wanted to finish this as quickly as possible. As Michael was looking at the list Lisa sent him, he ran into another cart. "Um, sorry; I didn't see you," as Michael lifted his eyes from his phone. He was looking at Taylor.

"Michael?" exclaimed Taylor, as she had not expected to see him out of all the shoppers here today.

"What are you doing here?" inquired Michael.

"I always come to this store. What about you? Guessing by the items you have in your cart, you're preparing for the wedding. Am I right?"

"Yup," replied Michael with a smile.

"Too bad it'll all go to waste," remarked Taylor with a light chuckle.

"Yeah..." stated Michael, as he was double-checking the list.

"All right, then. I should be going," explained Taylor.

"Wait. I forgot to tell you something."

"Is it about tonight?" inquired Taylor.

"Yes, I just wanted to make sure you understood your part," said Michael.

"You just want me to play the 'innocent bride', whose groom left her on her wedding day. Don't worry, I've been practicing for this," winked Taylor.

"All right then, good luck tomorrow," said Michael.

"You too and take care of Anna," replied Taylor.

Michael checked his phone clock. "It's already two, I gotta hurry," thought Michael, as he stood behind a line waiting for the cashier.

"You are late. Did something happen?" asked Lisa.

"No, it's just that some stuff were hard to find. Plus, the line was longer than usual," explained Michael.

"Is that so? Anyway, lunch's ready. Go dress and come to eat," remarked Lisa.

Michael hurried to his room and locked the door. He closed the bags after making sure everything was packed. Michael hid his bags under his bed. He then laid the clothes he would wear for the airport on his chair. Michael left his phone to charge and went down to eat his last meal with the family. "Dad? You're home early" noted Michael as he sat down in his seat.

"Yeah, I finished work early today," the family ate lunch together. Michael watched his family eating with smiles on their faces and wondered if he would ever miss them. "Probably not..." Michael thought, still eyeing everyone sitting before him.

"Already done?" asked Lisa.

"Yeah, I want to rest upstairs," explained Michael.

After locking the door, Michael went to his bad. He knew that he had to rest. Michael set an alarm for five. This should give him almost enough time to rest. While he was trying to sleep, the whole house was preparing for the big day tomorrow. "I feel sorry for them," thought Michael as he drifted away...

"MICHAEL, your alarm has been ringing for a while now," yelled Lisa, while knocking on the door. Michael quickly snoozed the clock and checked the alarm. 5:30PM; it was already late. Michael plugged all his electronic devices to juice-up before the trip. He also texted Anna and checked on her. The time was moving rather slowly for Michael. He was excited, yet anxious. His feelings were all over the place. But he knew that his objective was clear. Michael went to the café and bought a cup of coffee. Lucky for him, coffee had a strong effect on him. Its effect could last from morning, till 2AM. Michael thought that having a cup of coffee at 5:30PM would keep him awake till the next day.

Michael stayed at the café till around 8PM. He then returned as the sun started to set. His parents went to eat dinner. Michael told them he couldn't go with them. With almost four hours left, Michael made checking few last-minute checks. He made sure that everything was in place. Finally, Michael sat down at his desk and grabbed a piece of paper. He wrote a message for whoever read it first; then tied it to his ring. A ring that was given to him since he was thirteen. The ring resembled the family and meant a lot to his father. That's why Michael believed that he should leave it behind. After tying the message, Michael placed it on his desk.

Michael watched the clock as it was ticking and enjoyed the last few hours in his room. "All right, time to go..." he muttered, taking a long breath and then exhaling it. First, he made sure that his parents were asleep. Then he went down to check on the butlers.

"All clear."

Michael quickly retreated to his room, looked around one more time, and then grabbed his stuff. Watching him leaving was Isabella. She went to drink water. Isabella returned to bed as she thought this was just an illusion.

David was waiting outside. "All ready!" Michael ordered. David nodded. As they were on their way, David looked at

Michael through the front mirror. "You sure you wanna do this? This is your last chance to return," asked David.

"Yes, David. I made my decision long ago..." explained Michael.

Michael texted Anna, "You ready? We're on our way."

After almost ten minutes, Michael arrived at the park. "I'll go look for her," remarked Michael and David simply nodded.

As Michael was approaching Anna, he remembered the time he met her at midnight. And the countless times they met during the planning process.

"Anna!" He called out loud.

ANNA SAW MICHAEL APPROACHING HER; she immediately wiped her tears and put on a fake, pathetic smile. "What's wrong? Why are you crying?" inquired Michael.

"What? No. Why would you say that?" Anna showed some sorrow in her tone.

"Anna, my mom is a psychiatrist. Plus, I took a psychology elective, and have read a lot about facial expressions. Your face shows a person who was crying. A lot, in fact," explained Michael, and then continued, "So, can you tell me what's bothering you?"

"I just realized that I won't be able to return to this place, this country. I was raised here and lived a whole eighteen years right here," sobbed Anna, "And I'm afraid that I'll miss this place a lot. I mean, we will go to a new part of the world. I won't have anyone to comfort me or to protect me."

Up till now, Michael's view of Anna was different; he saw

her as a "tool". But now, he felt something strange. He knew Anna's nature. Michael grabbed Anna and hugged her.

"WHA—" snapped Anna

"You are wrong, Anna. You have me. And I will protect you no matter what," assured Michael. Anna felt the warmth from Michael. She closed her eyes and relaxed.

"Thanks Michael. Sorry for saying such things with you near me," sobbed Anna.

Michael smiled, and it was a real smile this time. For once, Michael experienced something that he never experienced with his family; true love. "Wipe your tears, Anna. David is waiting for us," remarked Michael, while giving Anna a handkerchief.

Anna wiped her tears under her glasses, then handed it back.

"Keep it with you," smiled Michael. Anna's usual face beamed up. "Yup, this face suits you better, a face full of joy and happiness," remarked Michael.

"All set," remarked Michael.

David nodded then headed straight to the airport. After a 20-minute ride, they arrived at the airport. Anna exited the car first. As Michael was exiting, David called on him, "Michael wait!" Michael stopped half way between the seat and the ground.

"Can I ask you one last thing?" inquired David.

"Um, sure," replied Michael.

"I was wondering, where are you even going?" asked David. Michael looked at David in the eyes, "Sorry David; it's better for you not to know."

"Good bye, Michael. Take care of yourself," said David

with a sigh. Michael smiled then went to help Anna with the luggage. Michael waved at David as he drove away.

"Come on Michael. Let's go," remarked Anna.

Both went to the counter to check in their luggage. "To Dubai," noted Michael as he handed the passports. After checking in, Anna went to have a cup of coffee; Michael tagged along.

"It's almost time," remarked Michael.

In the airplane, Michael was seated near the window. Anna was right next to him. Lucky for them, not one sat on the third seat by the aisle. "It's gonna be a long flight. We will arrive around 8PM the next day," explained Michael.

"By the way, what are we going to do with our phones? Are we gonna need them? After all, there is a big chance that they are tracked," inquired Anna.

"You can get rid of your phone once we arrive at the transfer airport. This way, we can distract them. But for me, I need to have it by my side all the time. Knowing my mom, she will call me claiming that she is on my side. I might have a chance to negotiate with her."

"I see. Then I will throw away my phone once we reach the airport."

UNITED

Lisa woke up by the sound of her alarm clock. "Wake up honey, it's almost time," she said softly.

Suddenly, the door was forced opened, "Mommy, Michael is not in his room!" barked Isabella.

"What?" snapped Larry. He immediately hopped out of the bed and rushed to Michael's room. After making sure that he indeed wasn't in there, Larry called the butlers and asked them to search around the mansion.

"I think I saw someone leaving the house last night. But I thought it was a butler," explained Isabella.

David was sleeping in his room. He didn't have enough time to sleep since last night. While searching, Lisa tried to call Michael's phone. "It's no use, his phone's out of coverage," explained Lisa.

"Damn it. Where could he be at such a time?" muttered Larry. The wedding was in two hours, and things were getting tense in the Walkers mansion. Since Michael's car was still here, Lisa assumed that he hadn't gotten far.

"Now what?" asked Lisa.

"We need to expand our searching area. Also, call Taylor's family," explained Larry.

"Got it," Lisa quickly dialed Sharlie's number. "Good morning, Sharlie."

"Ah, Lisa. How are you doing? Is Michael ready for his big day?"

"About that…" hesitated Lisa, and then continued. "He is missing."

"Oh no! Did you call the police?"

"Not yet… But more importantly, is Taylor here? Because we thought she might've escaped with Michael," explained Lisa.

"Yeah, she is preparing in the other room."

"Can you ask here about Michael?"

"All right, I'll go ask. Be in touch with you." Sharlie hung up and went to Taylor's room. "Taylor, I'm coming," said Sharlie, as she opened the door. "Michael is gone, and no one knows where he went. Any idea where he could be?"

"Michael is gone? I just met him yesterday while he was shopping," explained Taylor.

"So, you did it, Michael," thought Taylor. She was trying to hide her smile from Sharlie. "I honestly have no idea where he could be. I mean, we barely knew each other," remarked Taylor.

"I'll call Lisa, and you go tell James," ordered Sharlie.

"I guess we have no choice but to cancel the wedding," sighed James.

As Larry was trying to find the guest list, his phone rang; it was his old rival Richard. "Sorry, Richard, the wedding—"

"Never mind that," interrupted Richard, "my daughter is missing! We've been looking for her all morning!"

"What! Michael's also missing," exclaimed Larry.

"Do you think there is a connection between the disappearances of our children?" asked Richard.

"Dad look what I found," yelled Isabella, as she was marching through the hallway.

"The family's ring! Sorry Richard, I'll have to call you later. Meet me here with your wife."

"Wait—"

Larry hanged the call and grabbed the ring. He found a letter tied to the ring.

"Dear, (The person who is reading this). By the time you are reading this, I will be on a plane; a plane that is flying to a place far away from here. I'm assuming that the wedding was canceled at the last moment, and the house is in chaos. Well, that's nothing compared to the last 18 years of my life. As my father already knows, I had no free-will; my actions were based on his commands. While he was bragging about his son, I was taking all the damage. Ever wondered why I don't have any friends? It's because I wasn't allowed to be 'socially active'. To conclude, I'm sure that you all saw this day coming. Farewell; my former family. With 'Love', Michael."

Larry quickly went to the meeting room and showed the letter to Lisa. Meanwhile, Richard arrived with Rita. The four sat in the meeting room to analyze the problem. "We were at our summer house and returned this morning for Michael's wedding. When we arrived, Anna was already gone," explained Richard.

"I see, but do you think that they are connected somehow?" inquired Larry.

"I remember George mentioning something about Anna going with a friend. But I'm not sure whether he was Michael or someone else," remarked Rita.

"I just remembered!" snapped Larry, "Call Earl!"

"At once," replied the butler.

"Earl once told me before that he overheard Michael talking with Taylor in private."

"You called me sir?" Earl walked in, eyeing the other guests briefly.

"Yes, tell us what you heard that night; the conversation between Michael and Taylor," demanded Larry.

"I didn't hear the whole thing. But, I'm pretty sure that they mentioned something about canceling the wedding by not showing up," explained Earl.

"All right, you are dismissed." Everyone was in disbelief, especially Lisa.

"So, we can conclude that the reason for the escape was to avoid marrying Taylor. But, what about your daughter, Richard? Any reason for her to escape?" inquired Larry.

Richard's face turned pale. His face showed all his regrets up till now. "Actually, Anna was caught doing drugs. We told her to stay at home and attend rehab classes. I think she couldn't handle the rehab; therefore, she decided to escape. It's my fault for not being a good model to her," sobbed Rita.

Richard took Rita by his side for her to relax. "It's all right, honey. You didn't do anything wrong."

"So, both had a reason to escape," noted Lisa.

After wiping her made-up tears, Rita started to dial a number on her phone. "Hello, ma'am? Got a new chore for me?" inquired Lucas.

"Who's that?" asked Richard.

"He's Lucas; Anna's ex," explained Rita, while covering the phone with her hand. "Lucas, did you have a good look at that

Michael you told me of?" asked Rita as she tapped on the speaker icon.

"Yeah, he actually enrolled in the same rehab class as Anna. If I'm not mistaken, he had blackish hair, blue eyes. Wait, I think I took a photo of him; let me send it to you."

"All right, I'll be waiting for the photo."

"You got it," said Lucas, before Rita hung up the call.

"Well, as you heard, they might be working together after all," remarked Rita. Her voice was different from when she was faking her crying. As if she returned to her previous self. Lucas sent the photo. And even though it was blurry, the details were enough to make sure whether he was the Michael they wanted. "Is that your son?" asked Rita, while passing the phone to Larry.

It only took a glance from Larry to know that was Michael indeed. After taking a long breath, Larry spoke, "I'm afraid that he is our Michael."

"Let me see that," Lisa grabbed the phone from Larry's hand. She couldn't accept that it was her son. After looking closely, she finally admitted: "Yup, this is definitely Michael."

"Richard, Rita and Larry, despite your previous grudges, I want you to throw all what happened in the past, as I am requesting this. What do you say? We all put our hands together to search for our children," suggested Lisa.

The three looked at each other for a solid minute before anyone spoke. Finally, Richard stood up, "As much as I hated you Larry, I want my Anna to return. That's why I'll put my hand together with yours. And I'm pretty sure Rita shares me the same feeling."

Rita nodded silently. "So, Larry, what do you think?" asked Lisa.

"Fine. But I won't forget what Richard did to me in the past. I'll just forgive him for now," Spoke Larry like a true adult child, unable to set aside his past discourses.

"All right then, what's the plan?" inquired Rita.

"Hmm… I think we need to first locate them," explained Larry.

"But how?"

"I think I know how," remarked Richard and then snatched his phone from his right pocket. He then pointed at the back of his phone and continued, "Using a GPS tracker I planted in Anna's phone. They were last recorded at the airport; therefore, we can assume that they flew out of boarders."

"I see… but where to?" Inquired Larry, still puzzled by the accumulating events.

"For now, we will have to wait for them to land. Meanwhile, we will be in touch," explained Richard.

THE FLIGHT ARRIVED at Dubai airport around 9:30AM local time. Michael and Anna quickly went through the security immigration process and reached the arrivals hall. "How are we gonna reach the hotel?" inquired Anna.

"We'll use the metro," explained Michael, as he was searching for the way to the metro platform.

After walking for seven minutes or so, they arrived at a lone ticket counter. "Where to?" asked the woman.

"One way to the Emirates Towers Station please," answered Michael.

After getting the tickets, Michael and Anna went to the platform for the metro. "So, we finally made it…" remarked

Anna, reflecting on the rather bizarre circumstances that had lead to this very moment.

"Yup, we are finally free," the metro soon arrived, and they both hopped on at once.

"Since it's still early, why don't we drop our luggage then find something to eat?" recommended Michael.

"Yeah, I'm starving."

After a twenty-minute trip, they arrived at the station. It was a matter of exiting the station before they found their hotel. After checking in, Michael and Anna headed to their room. Michael went ahead of Anna as she went to the toilet downstairs. She arrived almost immediately after Michael; and the moment she entered the room, she noticed something. "There is only one bed, and it's a double."

"I tried talking with them, but it's no use," explained Michael, and then continued, "The whole hotel is booked. This is the only available room right now. They promised to manage a room for us. But we need to sleep here tonight."

"Is that so? I guess there is no other choice," Anna blushed ever so slightly.

"If you want, I can sleep on the couch and you sleep alone on the bed," offered Michael.

"No, no, it's all right," Anna's red cheeks grew more visible, for she had felt something deep inside.

"I'll just change my clothes, then we can go to have break-fast," remarked Michael.

As he was in the bathroom dressing, his phone, charging near their stationed luggage, rang. "Michael, your phone's ringing,"

"Who is it?"

"I don't know, let me check," replied Anna, as she was approaching the phone.

"It's your mom…"

"Finally!" muttered Michael, before exiting the bathroom.

"Stay quiet," whispered Michael. Michael tapped on the answer icon.

"Michael? Is that you sweetheart?" asked Lisa. Michael didn't respond.

"Michael? Are you all right? Answer me!" Lisa's attempts were rejected my Michael.

After a moment of silence, Michael spoke, "Exit the house."

"What?" hesitated Lisa.

"You heard me, go to a private place." Michael's voice was sharper than usual. Even Anna found his voice strange yet calm.

Lisa went outside, then returned to the call, "I am outside."

"All right. Now, what do you want?" asked Michael.

"What happened to you? Why did you suddenly disappear?" inquired Lisa.

"Mom, as much as I admire you, I don't think you can understand the situation. What's happening now is beyond your psychiatric level," remarked Michael.

Lisa paused for a moment, and then asked, "At least, where are you now?"

"Why are you asking?"

"I just want to help!"

"Brighton," Michael paused, gathered his breath, then continued, "You remember it, don't you? We went there three years ago."

"Oh yes, Brighton; such a lovely place. By the way, did you choose a university?" asked Lisa.

"Not yet, I still need more money," explained Michael, eyeing Anna.

"Then let me help you. I can transfer money to you via the bank app, and directly onto your card. How about that?" Lisa wanted to show Michael that she was on his side, which in a sense she was. Michael however was afraid that she could find his location while sending the money. But, since it's via the bank app, it won't be a problem, or so he had prayed.

"You would do that for me?" Michael suddenly changed his tone.

"Yes, I would do anything for my son. How much do you need?" asked Lisa.

"Hmm, let's see," mumbled Michael, "around £10,000, which is almost $13,000," replied Michael with a hidden grin on his face.

Lisa gasped, but tried to act normal. "Is that so? Fine, I'll transfer the money first thing tomorrow. Because it's almost midnight here. Speaking of which, what's the time there in Brighton?" Lisa was trying to see if Michael was lying. Michael quickly calculated the difference in time mentally, and then answered, "It's around eight in the morning here in Brighton. I was just about to eat breakfast."

Lisa knew he wasn't lying even though he was. Michael practiced the art of lying intensively. Eventually, he became so good at it that even a psychiatrist couldn't notice. "I see. All right then, I'm starting to feel a bit sleepy. Take care of yourself," Lisa hung up the phone.

Anna was astonished by what she just saw. She had no idea that Michael could do these things. "How did you do it?" She inquired with a puzzled face that still had traces of her recent blushing.

"Do what?"

"This whole thing; how did you manage to convince your mom that you were in Brighton and wanted tuition money?"

"Oh that, I just got used to doing these things. After all, I took psychology classes, and learned a lot from my mom," explained Michael.

"Is that so? Well, this sure backfired at her," noted Anna with a light chuckle.

"I guess you are right," replied Michael, as he was wearing his backpack.

"All right. Shall we go?"

TAG

After their last call, Lisa returned to bed, and Larry was waiting for her, "So, how did it go. Did he say anything about his whereabouts?"

"Oh indeed, he did... I told him that I'll be on his side. He immediately started to spill everything I needed," remarked Lisa.

"Excellent, as expected from my wife. So, where did he go?" asked Larry.

"Apparently, he went to Brighton."

"What else did he told you?"

"Can we discuss it tomorrow? I'm a bit sleepy. We were searching nonstop since the morning," explained Lisa.

"All right," sighed Larry.

Lisa was sleeping when a phone call woke her up. She peeked at her ringing phone, "An unknown number," thought Lisa. She wiped her eyes with her left hand while answering with the right hand.

"Hello? Lisa."

"Oh, hi Rita."

"We got a lead on where Michael and Anna are. The GPS got a signal for a few seconds before disappearing. But we managed to find the location. They were last tracked at Heathrow Airport," remarked Rita.

"Well, I managed to call Michael. And he said that he was in Brighton. So now we are sure that he is in England," explained Lisa.

"Nice work, I'm surprised that he told you his exact location."

"I kind of tricked him into thinking that I was on his side," smirked Lisa.

"Do you have any idea how to reach the rascals?" inquired Rita.

"Don't worry, I got some tricks up my sleeve." After hanging up, Lisa called for Earl. She was waiting for him in Larry's study room. Larry was already there when Earl knocked the door. "Come in," ordered Larry.

"You called me, Sir?"

"Yes, have a seat, Earl," offered Lisa.

"You see, we have a mission for you," remarked Larry.

"A mission?"

"Yes, we want you to go where Michael and Anna are. And stalk them for a couple of days before we decide on our next move," explained Lisa.

"Where are they?" asked Earl.

"Brighton," answered Larry.

"We'll prepare you with everything you need. You just need to follow them and report back to us. Also, keep this mission secret from everyone," remarked Larry.

"Understood. I'll get ready immediately."

As he was returning to his room, Earl passed by David. David heard a bit of the conversation. "Earl, can I ask you something?" called David.

"Yeah sure, what do you want?" Earl was younger than David and often thought of David as a role model.

"What did the masters ask you?"

"I'm sorry, David. I can't answer."

"Why not?"

"It's a secret mission. I can't talk about it."

"Come on Earl. You know me, don't you? I'm your friend, I won't tell anyone," David tried to convince Earl.

"All right," sighed Earl, and then narrowed his eyes, "But promise me that you won't tell anyone."

"Count on me."

"Larry wants me to go after Michael and stalk him," whispered Earl.

"Did they tell you were?" asked David, he was trying to maintain his coolness.

"He is in Brighton," answered Earl.

David's heart pounded, "When are you going?" fear colored his raunchy tone.

"I believe today," replied Earl.

"Is that so? All right then, good luck," David said, before walking past Earl.

"I gotta warn Michael" thought David, as he exited the house.

David checked Brighton's time zone. It was ten in the evening; he quickly dialed Michael's number.

"Come on, come on," muttered David.

"Um, hello?" spoke Michael.

"Michael!"

"David? What do you want? It's almost 1AM," inquired Michael, as he was wiping his eyes. Anna was sleeping right next to him, separated by a long pillow the hotel offered. Michael got off the bed and walked to the window.

"What? I thought it's ten in Brighton."

"Nah, it was a mislead. I'm in Dubai, and it's late. So, can you make it short?"

"Dubai, huh; good choice," remarked David, then continued. "Here is the thing…"

"I see. So, they bought my lie," smirked Michael.

"Don't worry, David, it's all part of the plan. Thanks for warning me, but I got everything under control," continued Michael.

"But what if they found out that you weren't in Brighton?"

"Leave that to me," replied Michael, then hung up the call.

"I promise that I'll protect you, Anna," muttered Michael.

As for David, he returned to his daily work. Earl was packing his bags when Larry opened the door.

"Sir!" snapped Earl.

"Earl, I couldn't mention this in front of Lisa but. I want you to return Michael no matter what. This wedding is very important to me and to this family. We can't just cancel it because Michael ran away. Your flight will depart in three hours. David will drive you to the airport," explained Larry, then took a deep breath, "I trust you to bring Michael back."

"Yes, Sir. I'll do my best," replied Earl.

Larry went afterwards to David. He was about to pick up Isabella from her club. "David!" David slid the car window open, "Yes, Sir?"

"I will pick Isabella. Meanwhile, I want you to drive Earl to the airport."

"You got it," said David before closing the car window. He parked the car near the front door waiting for Earl, who came shortly after; as both drove to the airport.

"All right, here we're," noted David, parking by the main entrance.

"Thanks, wish me luck," smiled Earl. David smiled back while nodding.

"Oh Sharlie, how are you?" spoke Lisa.

"I'm fine; thanks. I called to ask about Michael. Did you find him yet? James is getting on his nerves."

"Don't worry. We know where he is and already sent someone to pick him," explained Lisa.

"Is that so? Then I shall tell James," remarked Sharlie, "See you soon."

After ending the call, Lisa sent a message to Michael asking about the money. She already transferred exactly what he ordered.

"So, Michael… did you get the money?" texted Lisa.

Michael didn't reply. As Lisa was starting to get suspicious, she remembered the difference in time between them.

"He's probably sleeping," she thought with a shrug.

"Hey, Dad, can I ask you something?" inquired Taylor.

"Absolutely honey. What's on your mind?" replied James. It was dinnertime, and the family was enjoying their meal.

"It's about my wedding," noted Taylor.

"Look honey, they know where Michael is. It's a matter of time before he will return. Meanwhile, I want to relax and focus on your summer course."

"You know where he is?" snapped Taylor.

"Lisa told me he is in Brighton," answered Sharlie. Taylor was relieved. For a moment, she thought that Michael told them his real location.

"What if he didn't return? And what if he doesn't wanna marry me?" asked Taylor.

"It's not about him, it's about a wedding between two families. He has no other choice," explained James.

"Taylor why are you so pessimistic?" inquired Sharlie.

"Actually, about that…" Taylor grabbed her phone.

"Now!" texted Taylor.

"What about it?" As James was waiting for an answer, the bell rang.

"Who is it?"

"Sir, someone by the name of Paul is here to see you," reported the butler.

"Let him in," ordered Taylor.

"Hey, what's going on?" demanded James.

"Good evening everyone," said Paul, as he entered the room.

"Who are you?" asked James

"Allow me to explain," offered Taylor, as she stood up from her seat. "He is my real fiancé,"

Sharlie dropped her fork, "What do mean honey?" she asked. James remained silent in his seat.

"You see, Paul and I were supposed to be engaged a while ago. But thanks to some 'family shenanigans', I was engaged to

Michael. Of course, had I explained this to you any sooner, you would've just forced me to leave him."

"Is your father Glusto Valiant?" James fixed his eyes on Paul.

"Um, yes sir." replied Paul.

James smashed his hand at the table and stood up at once. "I won't allow a son of Glusto to marry my daughter," he barked.

"What's wrong honey?" asked Sharlie.

"Don't you remember? Glusto Valiant, the guy who bankrupted my company," explained James.

"Oh, you mean he was the one that was stealing from the company profit?" inquired Sharlie.

"But Dad, Paul has nothing to do with that. He wasn't even born back then!"

"Apparently you don't know the truth. Glusto was a loser who dropped out of college. I offered him to work under me for a good salary. Years went by, and the company started to lose profit. At first, we thought it was normal, until, I caught Glusto messing with the system. The company went downhill and never stood up again." James, sat down again, then continued, "It was thanks to the stolen money that he managed to create a family, and establish a rival company.

"Mr. James, I had no idea that my father did all that. I'm truly sorry," spoke Paul.

"Still, this has nothing to do with me marrying Paul," challenged Taylor.

"Weren't you listening? I won't repeat my last mistake and trust Glusto's child!" snapped James.

"You know, after all these years, I never thought I would say this; but you failed me, Dad. I thought you were a smart guy. A judge who can differentiate between his feelings and what is right," said Taylor with a sigh. Taylor switched her eyes to Sharlie.

"Honey, don't you think that you're being a bit unfair with her?" asked Sharlie.

"Taylor will marry Michael and that's final. I don't want to open this conversation again," James marched out, briefly crossing eyes with Paul. Sharlie followed him, and Taylor was left behind.

"I'm sorry Taylor, it's my fault all this happened," apologized Paul.

"Huh? It wasn't your fault. Don't blame yourself. I'll talk with them again. I'll see you tomorrow in class."

"All right, I'll be waiting." Paul approached Taylor. Both started at each other's eyes. Paul then kissed Taylor a goodbye kiss. Taylor placed her hands around Paul and closed her eyes. Paul felt something on his cheeks. "Are you crying?" Paul backed away from her.

"I'm sorry," Taylor wiped her tears with her clothes.

"All right, I gotta go; see you tomorrow," waved Paul. Taylor waved back at him.

"COME ON, Anna. We're running late," remarked Michael.

"Just a moment," replied Anna with a sleepy voice. She was yet to overcome her bad case of jet lag.

"Jeez, I didn't know you were a heavy sleeper," noted Michael.

While waiting for her, Michael checked his phone, "Good job, Mom," thought Michael, after checking his bank balance.

Anna was still dressing when Michael went downstairs to the reception.

"Sorry for taking so long to prepare," she later apologized.

Michael was waiting near the hotel's exit. "It's all right. While waiting for you, I asked about our university. We can take the metro to a station near the university. Then it's a matter of walking for five minutes or so," explained Michael.

"All right let's go. Hope we make it on time."

Michael and Anna wanted to adapt to the university environment as soon as possible. And there is no better way than attending the orientation week. Once they arrived, each took a separate path.

"We will meet here in two hours," noted Michael. Anna simply nodded. Michael went to the engineering building and searched for his instructors. Anna just walked around the place with no specific goal in mind. Both returned to the promised place after almost two hours.

"Are you done looking around?" asked Michael.

"Ya, what about you?"

"Same here. Wanna find somewhere to eat lunch?" offered Michael.

"Sure."

REDIRECTION

"Sir, my flight had just landed. Where should I go now?" called Earl.

"Hmm… First go to Brighton, then inspect all hotels for Michael and Anna. Call me once you find any leads."

"Give me the phone," spoke Lisa from the other side of the phone. "Listen Earl, in case you find their hotel, don't rush in. Just watch them from a distance and tell us their movement," explained Lisa.

She then returned the phone to Larry, "Don't fail us, Earl," said Larry before hanging up.

"What's next? What will you do once he finds them?" asked Lisa.

"Isn't it obvious? He will marry Taylor, then enroll in the university I handpicked for him," answered Larry.

The next morning, Larry woke up by eleven, and quickly texted Earl. Five hours had passed since his last update. Earl responded to the text immediately, "I was only able to cover half of the hotels. And neither Michael nor Anna were in any. I even asked for suspicious names, but still. I'll call you once I find anything," texted Earl.

"Apparently he still hasn't found them," remarked Larry.

"Is that so?" Yawned Lisa, as she was wiping her eyes.

"Couldn't you ask him about his hotel and save us some time?" asked Larry.

"He isn't that stupid, Larry. He'll obviously be suspicious if I asked him such questions," explained Lisa.

"All right, I'm off to work," Larry placed his fork, then stood up.

"Work? Isn't today a Sunday?" asked Lisa.

"Yeah, I've got a meeting," explained Larry, then took off.

Lisa went to the study room and locked the door. "Please answer..." hoped Lisa, as she was calling Michael.

"Hey, how is my big boy?"

"What do you want?" replied Michael.

"I just wanted to check on you. How's the weather? Are you eating well?" Lisa was trying to get any lead on where he was staying.

"Yeah, there is a restaurant near the hotel; I usually eat there."

"Near the hotel you say? Interesting..." Thought Lisa.

"Anyway, remember you are always welcomed back here," remarked Lisa.

"Good bye, mom," sighed Michael, and then hung up the call.

"A hotel with a restaurant nearby... Can you check for me?" asked Lisa.

"Sure, I'll call you once I find something," replied Earl.

Shortly afterwards, Earl called back, "I found it. There

were only a few hotels with restaurants nearby. And I already checked all of them expect one. I'm heading there right now."

"Excellent, text me once you are there," demanded Lisa.

"I'm almost there…"

Lisa immediately called Larry. "Honey, I have a meeting in five minutes. Anything important?" He asked, standing outside said meeting room.

"I think we found Michael. I'm just waiting for Earl's message," explained Lisa.

"What! How are you so sure?" inquired Larry.

"I called Michael, and he referred to a restaurant near his hotel. Earl said that he passed by all those hotels except for one, which he is heading for now."

Lisa's phone vibrated, "Oh, it's from Earl. Give me a moment to check it."

After checking the message, Lisa's voice changed, "He got us!"

"What?" Larry couldn't understand her tone.

"He tricked us!" Barked Lisa.

"I knew it. It was our fault for believing such an obvious lie," snapped Larry, then continued. "Call the Richards, we will meet together in two hour."

"Fine, and what about Earl?" asked Lisa.

"Tell him to return immediately," ordered Larry and then slammed his phone on the table. "Damn you Michael," he muttered.

"Earl, return," texted Lisa. She then called Rita and told them to meet after an hour.

～

"RICHARD, THEY TRICKED US," called Rita.

"What do you mean?" Asked Richard as he entered the room.

"Apparently, they're not in Brighton," explained Rita.

"What? Then what about the GPS signal?"

"What if it was just a transit? What if their final destination is far ahead?" Anna must've switched off her phone after arriving here. Therefore, the signal only picked the last location, Heathrow Airport," remarked Rita.

"I see. That makes sense. Anyway, what else did they say?"

"They'll meet us in an hour... their place."

Rita was in her bedroom while Richard went to Anna's room. Richard wanted to find anything that could be related to where Anna was. And while searching, Richard realized, "Wait a minute, how come Anna didn't show any symptoms of heavy drug usage?" he wondered. With that in mind, Richard drove to the rehab center and went to where they kept records of patients. "Hi, I'm Anna's father. I want to see my daughter's file, please," requested Richard.

"I'm sorry, we can't allow anyone to see the records of our patients," replied the woman standing behind the counter.

"But, I'm her father. Please, I need to check something," begged Richard.

"All right, but you can't take it outside this building," sighed the woman. She went to the back and searched for some time. "Got it," she soon said.

After getting hold of it, Richard quickly went through the papers. "Strange..." he thought. He took a photo, then handed the file back, "Thanks."

As he was exiting the center, Richard muttered in realization, "Shit, I'm late." He quickly drove back to pick up Rita.

"Where have you been?" asked Rita, as she has been waiting outside for some time now.

"Had to do something…" Richard spoke with a rather thick tone, which was foreign to Rita.

After arriving at Larry's house, David was outside welcoming them.

"All right, shall we start?" remarked Larry, after everyone was seated. "As you already know, they tricked us into thinking they were in Brighton," he noted, then continued, "We have no lead as to where they could be. Any ideas?"

"Why don't we ask the airport about the flights? They should know where they went," suggested Richard.

"Of course! Why didn't we think of that earlier?" agreed Lisa.

"All right, I'll text a friend that works there," offered Larry, scrolling through his contacts.

"Hi, how are you doing? I just wanted you to do me a favor. You see, my son traveled without telling us. Could you please check all the records of flights departing from Los Angeles. Thursday, around midnight," texted Larry.

"While we wait for him to respond, let's discuss who will go after him," noted Rita.

"We can send Earl, our butler," offered Lisa.

"But isn't he in Brighton? Even so, it will take precious time to wait for him to return here, then to go where they are," remarked Richard.

"I know someone who can help—Lucas," noted Rita.

"Yeah, that could work. He's Anna's friend, right?" approved Larry.

"Has your friend replied yet?" asked Richard.

"He said it will take some time to search for the flight," explained Larry.

While chatting, Larry's phone vibrated. "He replied!" Exclaimed Larry. Everyone was silent.

"So… where are they?" asked Rita.

"Dubai?" answered Larry, he himself puzzled by the choice of destination.

"But why Dubai?" inquired Lisa.

"It doesn't matter why. We have a lead now. Let us not waste any more time," explained Rita as she was dialing Lucas's number.

"Hey, Lucas. Are you free today?" asked Rita.

"Yes, I'm free. Any new missions?"

"What do you say to a free trip to Dubai?"

"Dubai you say? Yes, I would love to visit Dubai, heard lots of positive things about it."

"Great, however, this won't be a regular trip. I want you to search for Anna and bring her back."

"Bring her? How?"

"I don't care how. All I care about is for you to persuade her to return."

"All right, I accept your offer."

"Great, I will send you the flight information soon. Talk with your parents and send me your passport info," explained Rita.

"You got it—" Lucas hanged the call, repressing the urge to dance within his bedroom's walls.

"Done! Once he convinces Anna, Michael will have no choice but to return," explained Rita.

"All right then," said Larry, "we shall wait for further development. Meanwhile, let's all keep in touch."

~

"ALL SET, TIME TO GO!" muttered Lucas.

Lucas's flight was scheduled seven in the evening. Yet, he had already arrived at the terminal four hours in advance. He simply couldn't contain his excitement; both for the unpaid trip and winning back his treasured Anna. "I'm coming for you, Anna. And as for you, Michael, I won't let you have my beloved for yourself!" thought Lucas.

He sat patiently near the departure gate. And after the gate opened for passengers, he was the first in line. "Cool, first class," thought Lucas as he sat in his designated seat.

"Good evening, sir. Would you like to drink something?" asked the flight attendant.

"Yeah, I'll have a glass of wine."

"Coming shortly," remarked the flight attendant.

The gate was closed, and the plane departed shortly afterwards.

It was a 15-hour flight to Dubai International Airport. Upon landing, Lucas hurried to the front gate, as he was locating a vacant cab. "Where should I look first?" wondered Lucas. "First, I'll probably have to find something to eat." While immersed in his thoughts, Lucas gazed at an available taxi, and quickly hopped in.

"Where can I find something to eat?" He asked first thing after closing the door.

"Most restaurants are closed by now. But I think you might find something in Dubai Mall," answered the driver.

"I see, but first, I want to check into my hotel," remarked Lucas, as he was handing a paper with the address.

After a 30-minute ride, Lucas arrived.

"That'll be 110 Dirhams."

Lucas remembered that he didn't exchange any money, and grew anxious. "Will a credit card do?" he then inquired.

"Yeah, absolutely!"

"PHEW…"

After checking in, Lucas stood near the hotel's main entrance. He tried to find a second cab but didn't succeed. Then, Lucas glanced at a strange-looking building.

"What is that?" asked Lucas.

"Oh that, it's a metro station," replied the security guard standing near the entrance.

"Interesting, can it go to Dubai mall?"

"I think so," answered the guard.

Lucas walked to the station, then made his way to the ticket counter. "Hi, does this metro go to Dubai Mall?" inquired Lucas.

"Yes, do you want a one way or a return trip?" asked the lady.

"Um… I think I'll take a return trip," replied Lucas, then handed out his card. Lucas rushed to the platform as the train had just arrived. After five minutes, the metro arrived at The Dubai Mall station. Lucas had to walk a bridge for about fifteen minutes or so, before finally entering the mall. "So, this is Dubai Mall…"

Lucas chose a random restaurant and sat near the exit. His seat allowed for a view of the people walking outside the restaurant. Lucas ate and then paid the bill. He then took out his phone to message Rita. Suddenly, right by him, walked Michael and Anna. Lucas immediately took a menu and covered his face. He tried to peek from above and saw them walking past the restaurant.

"Phew, that was close," thought Lucas, as he exited the restaurant at once, following the two. While trying to maintain his distance, Lucas tried to hear what they were saying. He then realized that they are heading for the metro station. He waited for them to purchase a ticket, then asked the man behind the counter, "Where are they going?"

"You mean the couple just now? They went to the Emirates Towers Station," answered the man.

"Lucky me!" thought Lucas. He thanked the man and went right after them. Lucas was heading for the same station as Michael and Anna. In the metro, Lucas sat in another cart, but had an eye on them. He waited for them to leave first. Apparently, both hotels were on the opposite sides of the street, each on one side. Lucas followed them to the other side of the road just to take note of the hotel's name.

"So is that where you are, Michael…" grinned Lucas, as he was walking back to his hotel.

EXPOSED

Two weeks had passed since Lucas sat his feet in Dubai. He was watching Michael and Anna every day. When they left the hotel, and when they returned. "Good morning, Sir. How may I help you today?" asked the receptionist.

"Yeah, I forgot my keycard inside the room, and now I can't enter my room," explained Lucas.

"Absolutely, but first, may I know your last name?"

"It's Walker; Michael Walker," replied Lucas. The receptionist started to type something, then handed a new card, "There you go, Mr. Walker. Make sure to return it once you find your card," Lucas nodded and took the card.

"I didn't think it would be this easy," he thought.

Lucas found the room and tapped on the sensor with the card; the door was opened. "Damn, and here I thought my room was better," He then realized that he didn't know when the two would return. "I guess I have to risk it all," he sat at the sofa and wondered, "Will Anna come first, or will it be Michael? Or, perhaps both will come at the same time?" Lucas knew there was no time to retreat.

. . .

"FINALLY!" thought Lucas as he heard a 'beep' from the sensor near the door. "Here it is," he muttered. The door slowly opened, and someone entered. Lucas couldn't tell since he was in another room. He could only hear one pair of footsteps. Therefore, only one had returned. A moment later that person entered the room.

"Lucas!" gasped Anna.

"Surprised?" Lucas remained seated on the sofa. Anna froze in her place.

"How did you find me… is that what you wanted to ask?" Lucas finally stood up. Anna slowly grabbed her phone from her pocket.

"No need for that. I just want to talk to you," explained Lucas.

Anna took her hands out of her pockets and then rested her back against the wall. "What do you want?"

"Why did you escape? And why with him?"

"Why do *you* care?" replied Anna.

"It's just that you deserve something better than him. Something better than living here," Lucas paused to take a breath then continued, "Come with me! I promise you, I'll make you happy. Leave Michael here and come with me!" Anna said nothing. Instead, she was looking at him, deep into his eyes.

"What do you think?" asked Lucas.

"You don't get it, do you? The reason I came here is because I hate living where I was. I wanted to get as far as possible from that place," explained Anna.

"But, why? What happened?" inquired Lucas.

"I was falsely accused of taking drugs. Can you imagine? Everyone blaming you for something you never did," Anna started to tear.

"So, what? You already proved to them that you were clean. There's no need to go to the other side of the world just because of that," remarked Lucas.

"That wasn't the only reason—you know, why even bother telling you. You won't understand either way. Now get out before I call the cops!" demanded Anna.

"Are you sure about that? You really think this is the right choice? If yes, I won't stand between you and your happiness," Lucas assured with a sigh. He then walked past Anna and left the room. Before exiting the hotel, Lucas passed by the reception and returned the card. Entering through the front entrance was Michael. Michael returned because Anna took so long looking for her wallet.

"Take care of Anna," whispered Lucas as he passed by Michael.

Michael recognized that voice, he turned his face, but Lucas was already gone.

RICHARD WOKE UP EARLY, earlier than Rita, that is. Richard skipped work as he wanted to continue his private search. He checked the photo he took yesterday.

"The drug... I've seen it before, but where?" wondered Richard.

After drinking his morning coffee, Richard sat in his car and tried to recall the chain of events that had led to today.

"Olivia!" snapped Richard.

Richard used to visit Olivia with Rita. And every time, he would spot that same drug stashed. Richard quickly drove to Olivia's house. "Olivia, open up!" yelled Richard, while knocking rapidly at the door.

"What's with all the yelling? I was trying to sleep," Olivia opened the door to find Richard standing with his arms crossed.

"Can I talk to you for a moment?" requested Richard.

"Um, sure. Come in," offered Olivia.

Richard was searching with his eyes for that drug. "Found it!" He muttered.

"Hey, don't touch that!" ordered Olivia, but it was too late.

"I knew it," spoke Richard and fixed his eyes on Olivia. "I'll ask only once. Did you, or did you not, give Anna these drugs?" Richard asked with a deep voice.

Olivia shivered, "Anna? No, why are you asking?" she hesitated.

"It's simple, I found the same exact drugs in her room. They were also wrapped the same way. Does this answer your question? Now answer mine," ordered Richard.

Olivia sighed, "I wasn't the one who gave her the drugs."

"Who gave her the drugs?" asked Richard calmly.

"There is no way I could tell you!" insisted Olivia.

Richard grabbed Olivia by her neck, "Listen, don't play games with me. Anna ran away because of you. Now, will you speak, or should I force you to?"

"Fine, fine. Take your hand off me!" snapped Olivia. "It was Rita. But I swear, I never thought Anna would escape. All Rita wanted was some attention from you!" yelled Olivia then stopped to catch her breath.

Richard's heart was pounding like crazy. He couldn't

gather his thoughts; yet, he tried to act normal. "So that's what happened?" He asked calmly.

"Yes, that's what happened," admitted Olivia. She started to feel guilty. The fact that she just destroyed a family couldn't escape her thoughts.

"Umm, I know it's too late. But can I do anything to help?" inquired Olivia.

"No, you've done enough. I'll handle it from now on," noted Richard, as he was ready to leave.

Olivia couldn't even lift her eyes off the floor. She felt a huge weight on her body. Richard started his car and went directly to Rita.

RITA WAS in the bathroom doing her morning routine when her phone rang. It was placed near her bed. Rita rushed to the phone and answered, "Hello?"

"Hi, ma'am, hope it's not a bad time," replied Lucas.

"It's fine. More importantly, what happened regarding your assignment? Any new updates?" inquired Rita.

"About that… I'm sorry, but I quit—"

"Wait, what?" Rita interrupted.

"I can't do this anymore. I think Anna deserves to live the life she wants. Neither one of us have the right to decide her future."

"What are you even saying? Did something happen there? Tell me!" barked Rita.

"Thanks for everything," remarked Lucas before hanging up.

Rita slammed the phone on to the table near her bed,

"Damn it, that Lucas. Thinking he can just quit." She tried to prioritize her thoughts. For starters, Rita doesn't really care whether Anna returns or not. After all, she was the one who pushed Anna to escape. With that being established, Rita returned to the bathroom.

Not long after, Rita went to have her morning coffee. She sat in the study room that she shared with Richard. "I should probably call Lisa," thought Rita, then dialed Lisa's number.

"Hi, Lisa, I wanted to inform you that the plan failed."

"Why? What happened?"

"Lucas just called. He said he quits. I don't know what got into him, but he seemed serious."

"Hang up, NOW!"

Rita turned her face to see Richard standing by the door with a pale face

"Hello? You in there?" asked Lisa.

"I said hang up," demanded Richard.

Rita at once hanged the call, then placed the phone on the table. "What's the matter, honey? Weren't you supposed to be at work?" She began to sweat in anticipation of the inevitable confrontation about to unfold before her very eyes. She was chiefly mortified of that emotionless face Richard had on. Meanwhile Richard remained silent as he locked the door behind him.

"Where should I start? Hmm... let's see, how about that night?" spoke Richard, then continued, "The night Anna visited that new campus."

Rita's blood rushed to her heart, and she started to shiver ever so slightly. "Y-you mean the night we found Anna's stash?" she hesitated.

"Let me correct you right there. It's the night *I* found that stash. You didn't find but rather hid the drugs in question," remarked Richard while grabbing the drugs out of his pockets.

"What are you saying, honey? I don't get it."

"I see what you are doing here; just give me a sec." Richard dialed a number on his phone as Rita was shivering in her seat.

"Hello?" spoke Olivia.

"Hi, Olivia, I'm here with Rita and she claims that she has no idea of what happened that night. Could you please remind her?" requested Richard.

"You couldn't keep your mouth closed, could you Olivia!" snapped Rita.

"I—" Richard hanged the call before Olivia could justify anything.

"Moving on," said Richard, "I shall give you ten seconds to explain yourself before I go berserk."

"I—I'm really sorry. I just couldn't accept the fact that you treated her better than me. But I never intended to let Anna esc—"

"All right, time's up," remarked Richard.

After taking a long breath, Richard resumed talking, "Do you have any idea what you did to Anna's life? DO YOU?" barked Richard. "You ruined her life. Not only did she escape but she also skipped on her education. Is that what you wanted? To ruin her life so that you could have a better one? Let me tell you this one thing, Anna will hate you for the rest of her life. Every decision she will make from now on will be because of your brainless idea," Richard clenched his fists and tried to calm down. Rita was crying, and Richard still assumed his authoritative posture as he stood before her.

"I'm sorry... I really am..." cried Rita.

"Don't apologize. Tell that to Anna. Although I doubt she'll forgive you. In fact, I doubt she will forgive either of us," Richard held back his sorrow and tears, the best he could. "I'm not sure if you know how things work in such cases, but I'm filing for divorce."

"Honey, please, consider what you are saying!" snapped Rita.

"You should've thought about that before... RUINING my daughter's life!" snapped Richard then left the room to call Larry.

"LARRY, RITA CALLED," remarked Lisa.

"And?"

"She said the plan failed. But, something happened, and she hanged the call suddenly. I'm worried..." explained Lisa.

"Is that so, I guess we're gonna have to find a replacement —" Larry's phone rang, "I gotta take this."

"Who is it?" asked Lisa.

"Richard."

"Hey, Richard, what's up?" asked Larry.

"Can I talk with you privately? Away from Lisa."

"Sure, just let me exit the room," remarked Larry, eyeing Lisa.

"All right, what do you want?"

"I'll try to make things short, since you are a busy man,"

noted Richard. Larry then listened to the whole thing—about what happened that damned night.

"I see what's going on. I'm sorry for what happened to you. By the way, you sure about divorcing Rita?"

"What would you do? I mean, she planted drugs in her daughter's room. Plus, she was quiet the whole time. I lost my faith in her," explained Richard.

"I guess you got a point there. Fine, I'll help you—"

"One more thing, please keep this away from Lisa. It's not that I don't trust her. I just want this to be between the two of us," remarked Richard.

"All right. Also, what will you do now? About Anna?" asked Larry.

"I'm not sure anymore. I doubt she will believe me in the first place; but I'll try to call her tonight."

Larry returned to his waiting wife. "So? What did he want?" inquired Lisa.

"He just asked about a problem he faced at work," explained Larry.

"I see." Lisa could easily tell when Larry lies. It's as if she can read his thoughts.

While eating lunch, Larry kept silent. "What's wrong? Still worried about Michael?" she asked.

"Yup, gotta figure out how to reach him," replied Larry. Both then continued their meal in utter silence.

"All right, gotta go," spoke Larry as he stood up.

"Where to?" inquired Lisa.

"I have a tough case ahead, so I'll be in my study ," explained Larry then left at once.

"Hey, Rita, is everything all right?" texted Lisa; she knew that Larry was hiding something.

"Richard found out," replied Rita.

"What exactly did he find out?"

"Everything…" texted Rita.

"Everything?"

Rita then stopped responding to Lisa's texts.

DILEMMA

Almost a month had passed since Richard confronted Rita. Things were settled as both went to court. And with Larry's help, Richard won the custody of Anna. Rita took her belongings and left in shame and disgrace. She went to her parents' house. As for Anna, she was by now settled in Dubai. Both she and Michael took their time in exploring the city since the university won't start till the end of August. Richard tried to call Anna several times before, but to no avail. Anna would just decline any call from either her parents.

"Where should we eat dinner?" inquired Anna.

"Hmm, how about that fancy restaurant near the beach?" suggested Michael.

"Sure, let's give it a try," remarked Anna.

It was 7:30PM, yet both were starving since they skipped lunch. The weather changed a lot since they arrived. It's not that hot, and a cool breeze blew by at night.

"A table for two please," spoke Michael.

"Absolutely, right here," replied the waiter.

"How about here?" asked the waiter. It was a nice table by

the window. Anna nodded, and so did Michael. After settling, both ordered their usual food; the dishes they'd yearned for since leaving their home country.

"Nice view," remarked Anna. Michael nodded smoothly. The atmosphere was quiet; and both had nothing to say.

"Sorry for waiting, here you go," said the waiter, as he placed the appetizers.

While eating, Anna's phone rang. "Really? They just won't stop," she thought while tapping the 'reject call' button. Shortly afterwards, the phone rang again. "Urgh, fine, I'll answer," muttered Anna. "Sorry, I gotta take this," spoke Anna before exiting the restaurant.

Anna walked till she had a clear view of the sea. She then tapped on the 'Answer' button. "What!"

"I haven't talked to you in like two months, and this is how you greet me?" laughed Richard. Anna didn't respond.

"Look, Anna, no need for you to reply, just listen to what I have to say," remarked Richard.

"Fine, say what you want. But make it quick," sighed Anna.

"After you escaped, I felt like it was my fault. So, I started to sniff up any evidence that would prove otherwise. Then it hit me, the drugs we found were the same as those Olivia had. After digging even deeper, I reached her and proved my point. After that Olivia spilled the whole thing," explained Richard, then paused.

"And?" asked Anna.

"The one who planted the drugs was your mother, Rita," remarked Richard.

Anna gasped, "So mom planted the drugs!"

"I know it's hard to believe, but that's the truth," sighed Richard, then continued, "After learning the truth, I returned home and asked Rita whether she did it or not. After making sure, I asked her to move out. We got divorced…"

Anna remained silent and continued walking along the seaside.

"So please, can you return? We can live together and start again. I know what we did was unforgettable; but I really thought that my only daughter was an addict," offered Richard.

"I don't know what to say. I really don't think I can respond to what I just heard. It's just so much information to process."

"It's all right. You don't need to decide now. By the way, did you enroll in any university?" inquired Richard.

"Yeah, and I'll start in two weeks," replied Anna.

"Phew, so you still have time. Listen, think about what I just told you. I'll call you back in a week to get an answer. Stay safe, love ya!"

Anna then hanged the call, as she stood still in her place. She was facing her greatest dilemma yet. "Michael or my father… LA or Dubai…" Anna kept wondering for a while before realizing she was late. She thus rushed back inside, seating herself and reaching for the fork and knife laid before her.

"What's wrong? Who was it?" inquired Michael.

"Don't worry, it's no one," replied Anna with a fake smile. Michael realized something was going on; but kept silent. After eating their fancy meal, both paid their half of the bill. They then headed directly back to the hotel. Along the way, Anna was silent and showed a dejected face.

Upon arriving, Anna went to directly bed; she didn't even brush her teeth or take a shower as she usually would.

Michael had no other choice but to watch from behind and analyze.

THE FOLLOWING DAY, Anna began to feel a tad better. She woke earlier than every other day; opting for a quick shower while Michael was still asleep.

"Good morning Michael," Anna was waiting for Michael to open his now cracking eyelids.

"Well, you are early," remarked Michael, as he was stretching his arms above his head.

"Maybe because I went to bed early," explained Anna, then continued, "What should we do today?"

"Hmm, how about that Anime store you always wanted to visit?" suggested Michael.

"Oh, you remembered!" smiled Anna.

After getting dressed up, Michael was ready to start his day. And after eating breakfast near the hotel, both went to the station. Anna has six days now to decide about what Richard had offered her...

THE PROPOSED WEEK WENT BY, and Anna was yet to decide. With a week left to the start of her semester, Anna felt that her options were getting limited. Michael was at the compact supermarket near the hotel buying some essentials, while Anna stayed at the hotel.

"That'll be seventy five Dirhams," remarked the cashier.

Michael handed him hundred Dirham. After returning the change, the cashier asked Michael to donate. Michael slipped a ten Dirham bill through the donation box, then walked out.

Ever since that night in the restaurant, Michael have been preoccupied with the ominous call. "Who was it? Could it be her parents? Perhaps Lucas?" Michael wondered about the identity of the caller as he arrived at the hotel's lobby.

"Good morning, Sir." Waved the receptionist.

Michael waved back at him and walked to his room. And as he was about to tap the door sensor with the keycard, he heard Anna's voice through the door. Michael placed his ears on the door and tried to catch anything.

"Yes, Dad, I made my decision," answered Anna.

"Decision?" thought Michael.

"I'll return home..." continued Anna.

Michael's heart pounded. "What? Did she say that she's returning? What's going on?" He thought, waiting for Anna to end her call before opening the door.

"What took you so long?" asked Anna.

"Sorry, I took a quick walk around the block," answered Michael.

"In this weather? It's like hundred five degrees out there!"

"Well, I gotta keep up my shape."

Michael went to take a shower while Anna waited for her turn.

"What should I do? Should I tell her?" He wondered as the water rained all over his trembling body. He was above all confused. Why did Anna call her father? After getting out of the bathroom, Michael locked his eyes onto Anna's eyes. Without noticing, he showed a fearful look up his eyes.

"What?" asked Anna.

"I'm sorry, I got some shampoo into my eyes." Michael

tried to remain his usual self. He waited for Anna to take her shower and sat in the sofa.

"Before we go, I want to talk about something," remarked Michael.

"Sure…" Anna sat down near Michael.

"You know, exercising wasn't the only thing I did this morning," spoke Michael.

"What do you mean?" inquired Anna.

"Let me rephrase that. Anything happened to you this morning? Anything 'special'?" asked Michael.

"Let me guess, you heard everything?" sighed Anna. Michael simply nodded. "It's not what you think it is. I can explain," hesitated Anna.

"Then do so," offered Michael.

Anna explained the whole thing, Michael then stood up, "So you are telling me that after all that we did, you want to return?"

"I didn't know my mom was responsible for the drugs. And since my dad divorced her, I can live with him once again."

"Don't you get it? The only reason he wants you to return is because he needs you. You are his trump card."

"Trump card? What do you mean? He just wants to live with his only daughter," Anna was lost. She didn't know who to believe.

"I know Richard, my dad always told me about him; he's an evil man. Look, I did my research, and he will do anything to reach his goal. And now, he needs you to reach that goal. I doubt that he even divorced your mom," Michael stopped to gather his breath.

Anna took off her glasses to wipe her tears. "I never

thought you'd be like this, Michael. After all, you're just jealous. You realized that I will return to my caring father while you'll stay here alone with no family."

"Please tell me you are joking, I only escaped because I didn't want my family to control me. That's why I'm warning you about returning to them," explained Michael.

"Why do you believe that all families are the same as yours? My father treated me like a princess, until my mom planted those drugs that is. And now... she is gone. I don't think you'll understand the meaning of a 'true family'. By the way, my flight is tomorrow morning," Anna started to lose hope in convincing Michael.

"Let me ask you this. Why do you think I care whether you stayed or went? The answer is simple: I care about you! Come on, let's go eat breakfast," remarked Michael, then went ahead of her. Anna wiped her tears and walked after him.

Both walked in awkward silence to the restaurant near the hotel. There, they sat at their usual table and ordered while still not making eye contact, let alone talking to each other. While eating, Michael started to feel bad about what he said earlier; he only wanted Anna to stay with him. Shortly afterwards, the waitress arrived with their dishes. No one touched the food as if they were about to say something to each other.

Michael took a long breath then broke the silence, "Um—"

"Michael," interrupted Anna, "I want to say something. I've been thinking about what you said. And... I think—" Anna stopped talking.

"Anna?"

Anna's fork fell on the ground, while her head landed on the table, right into the steaming plate.

"Anna! Are you okay?" snapped Michael, getting off at once.

"Sir? What's going on?" asked the waitress.

"I don't know, call the ambulance!" yelled Michael while tapping on Anna's shoulders.

"Hey, can you hear me?" cried Michael. Once again, Anna didn't respond. Michael lifted her head up from the plate. "She's unconscious…"

The whole restaurant was staring at Michael as he his chair near Anna's and then sat down while laying Anna's head on his lap. While waiting, Michael wiped the food off Anna's forehead and hair. He sat like that for ten minutes, before the ambulance arrived.

"Over here!" called Michael.

"What happened?" asked the paramedic.

"She suddenly lost conscious," answered Michael.

The rest of the team then came to pick Anna. And along Michael, Anna was taken to the hospital.

"Anna, what were you about to say?" wondered Michael. His eyes then started to tear. Michael closed his eyes to relax; and while regretting what he told her, the paramedic tapped his shoulders, "She's waking up."

Michael opened his eyes to see Anna's mouth moving. "Anna!" He tried to get near her head.

"Where am I?" trembled Anna.

"You passed out, and we are on our way to the hospital," explained Michael.

"Hospital? Who are you anyway?"

FORGOTTEN

THE BLOOD RUSHED TO MICHAEL'S HEART AND HEAD AT ONCE, "What are you saying? It's me, Michael."

"Michael? Never heard of this name before..." trembled Anna.

"What's going on? Why can't she remember me?" yelled Michael, his eyes started to tear after having dried not five minutes ago.

"Anna, can you move your hands?" asked the paramedic.

"I... I don't feel my right arm," replied Anna as she moved her left arm.

"Was afraid of this..." muttered the paramedic.

"What do you mean?" Michael stepped in.

"I'm not a professional in this field, but I believe your girlfriend had a stroke."

"Anna..." thought Michael.

MICHAEL WAS STANDING outside Anna's room. Soon the door was pushed open, and Michael saw a doctor leaving. "Good morning, my name is Hamad and I will be responsible for Anna's diagnosis.

"Please doctor, do anything to bring her back," begged Michael.

"You see; brain strokes are usually fatal. After running some tests, we believe that Anna's left-brain was affected. The left-brain controls the right side of the body, while the right-brain controls the left side," Hamad paused before continuing, "Depending on which side is affected, a brain stroke can have different symptoms. In Anna's case, the right side of her body is completely paralyzed, and she lost part of her memories."

"Is there any cure?" asked Michael.

"Unfortunately for Anna, a blood vessel in her brain busted. As a result, it caused what we call 'hemorrhagic stroke'. While rare, it appears to be more fatal. The thing with this type of strokes is that the more she waits the worse it will get. It has already been forty minutes since she first lost conscious, am I right?"

Michael nodded. "So, are you saying that there is no cure?"

"Too bad there isn't. And even if there was, it's too late. While taking samples, I noticed that she had an early stage of diabetes, which increased her chances of getting a stroke," remarked Hamad with a sigh.

Michael closed his eyes; he then opened them and asked, "Doctor, can I ask you for a favor?"

"Sure, what do you want?"

"I want to have a moment alone with Anna. Can you please ask the nurse to leave us alone?" requested Michael.

"All right," Dr. Hamad went inside the room to talk with the nurse while Michael stood behind him. After he had left with the nurse, Michael was at last alone with Anna. He waddled to her bed and slowly bent his knees to reach her head level. "I'm sorry Anna. It's all my fault," whispered Michael. Anna appeared to be asleep, and despite that Michael proceeded:

"Because of me, you had to leave your home country. Because of me, you wasted your chance to enroll in a good university. And because of me, you will die away from everyone you loved and knew..."

"That's not entirely true," muttered Anna with a faint voice.

"Anna, sorry for waking you up," snapped Michael.

"T—the last thing you said, isn't true," struggled Anna.

"What do you mean?"

"It's true that I don't remember who you are. But, deep inside, a voice tells me that you were with me the whole time." Anna paused, "That voice reminded me that I'm not alone. I never was." Anna had some problems with pronunciation since she had woken up. Michael figured that it was because of the stroke.

"I'm sorry, I really am. If only you stayed back in L.A., none of this would've happened," apologized Michael.

"You know what else that voice tells me?" asked Anna as she grabbed Michael's shirt with her left hand.

"WHA—" Before Michael knew it, his lips were touching Anna's. Michael closed his eyes; his heart pounded like crazy. But once he remembered that Anna was dying, his heartbeats slowed down, and tears rolled down his cheeks. At this moment, Michael wished the time would stop, for he wanted to live this moment forever. Suddenly, Michael heard the device near Anna's bed beeping. It then started to beep rapidly before settling on a long beep. The screen showed a straight green line.

Michael immediately backed off, "Anna? Anna!" cried Michael. He then rushed to the exit and started yelling, "Doctor!"

Dr. Hamad came running to the room with him were a crew of nurses.

"What happened to Anna?"

"I'm sorry son, her time is up," Dr. Hamad reached and hugged Michael's trembling body.

"ANNA!" cried Michael while Hamad was trying to comfort him.

Michael wiped his tears, then walked to Anna's bed. He kissed her forehead and wiped the tears off her cheeks. He took Anna's glasses off her cold face and watched as Hamad covered her slowly stiffing body.

"Good bye, Anna," muttered Michael, as he slid her glasses in his pocket.

MICHAEL ARRIVED AT HIS HOTEL. His face was pale, and he had red puffy eyes from crying. "What's up Michael, where is Anna? Wasn't she with you?" asked the guard by the door. Michael looked deep into his eyes, "She is not here anymore…"

In the room, Michael stood by the entrance, flashbacks started to appear in his already preoccupied mind. "Anna…" muttered Michael, before opening the door. Michael placed Anna's glasses on the nightstand near the bed; before throwing himself on Anna's side. He was tired; so tired in fact that he couldn't close his eyes. The only thing that helped him relax was Anna's nostalgic scent on her pillow. Without realizing, Michael had slept for about ninety minutes. He'd already booked a flight back to LA that would depart the same time as Anna's original flight.

Michael packed two bags: one for him, and the other was for Anna; he wanted to return Anna's belongings back to her family. While packing, Michael found Anna's diary. He opened it out of curiosity, and something fell out of it; it was his handkerchief. Anna kept it after Michael had given it to her. Michael hid the diary in his back pocket, then resumed packing.

It was still 5PM when Michael zipped both bags; he still had fourteen hours till the flight's departure. Michael sat the bags near the door, then changed his clothes. He wanted to go somewhere to relax and think clearly. Michael then remembered his favorite place back home. He waved at the taxi waiting near the entrance.

"Are there any zoos nearby?" asked Michael.

"Yes, there is one twenty minutes away," answered the driver.

Michael went to the local zoo, a place where he could think straight. There he searched for the crows cage and sat near them. "You are the only thing that's left for me," remarked Michael while looking at the crow's eyes. Michael then grabbed Anna's diary out of his pocket, and started reading, from the very first page.

"Sir, the zoo is closing soon," noted the guard.

"Oh, I'm sorry. I lost track of time," Michael hid the diary and moved on. Lucky for him, he found a taxi waiting by the zoo entrance.

"To Dubai mall, please," remarked Michael. The driver nodded.

Michael wanted something to eat since he couldn't eat breakfast this morning. "I will need someone to finish Anna's death papers," thought Michael. He then sent a message to an old friend.

Michael arrived and walked around searching for a restaurant. He then walked by a restaurant he enjoyed; it was the very first restaurant Michael went to since he arrived in Dubai.

"Oh, you're from last time. Where is your girlfriend?" asked the waiter.

"Time broke us apart."

"I'm sorry to hear that. Where do you wanna sit?" asked the waiter.

"Over there," pointed Michael.

The waiter nodded and grabbed a menu with him to the table. Michael sat down with a wall behind him, just like before.

"I'll have what I had last time," requested Michael.

"Absolutely."

Shortly afterwards, Michael saw Lucas near the restaurant's entrance. The waiter pointed at Michael's table, and Lucas walked to him. "Thanks for coming," remarked Michael.

"What do you want? And where's Anna?" asked Lucas.

"First, I want you to take a seat. I also want you to take a long deep breath before I begin talking." Lucas sat down accordingly, then took a long breath, just like Michael ordered.

"Anna is no longer here," spoke Michael.

"What do you mean?" inquired Lucas.

"She is dead. Now, I want you to choose your next words carefully," noted Michael.

"WHAT!" Lucas was about to turn berserk but saw the people around him staring.

"Calm down and listen to what I have to say…" Michael started from when he overheard Anna talking with Richard. Lucas didn't blink; his eyes were fixed on Michael.

"Is that so?" muttered Lucas, "Why did you tell me all of that? You know well that I have nothing to do with either one of you."

"You are wrong, Lucas. I told you to meet me here because I have a favor to ask you; actually, me and Anna both have a favor to ask," explained Michael.

"And what could it be?"

"Tomorrow morning, I will return to LA. Can you finish Anna's death papers? You can contact the embassy for details. I'm sure that she would want to be buried in the home country. Can you do this for Anna?" requested Michael.

"Leave it to me. In return, I want to attend her funeral," demanded Lucas.

"Sure, buddy," smiled Michael.

"I'm sure Anna would be happy to see us working together," remarked Lucas.

"I bet she would…"

Shortly afterwards, the waiter arrived with the food. Michael was eating while Lucas kept staring at him.

Michael peeked at his phone clock, "It's already nine!" he exclaimed.

"When's your flight?" inquired Lucas.

"I believe it's around seven thirty," replied Michael before taking a sip of water.

"Oh, I just remembered. I need you to come back to my hotel," remarked Michael

"Why?"

"I need to hand you Anna's documents."

Michael then paid the bill and headed back to his place. Lucas tagged along.

As Lucas was entering through the main gate, his eyes met with the receptionist. "Shit!" Lucas muttered.

"Um, can I wait for you outside?" he asked.

"Why?"

"I wanna get some fresh air. You go bring the papers, and I'll wait here," Lucas wanted to avoid meeting with the receptionist, especially after he tricked him into getting the room key.

"All right, if you insist. I'll be back soon," remarked Michael.

Lucas stood outside by the door and thought about what had happened to Anna. "Poor Anna, she had to suffer till her last breath. Hope she can rest now; I'll make sure she does," Lucas then started to regret not forcing Anna to return with him. While swimming in his thoughts, Michael approached him from behind.

"Whoa, that was fast," said Lucas.

"Yeah, I sort of prepared the documents in advance."

"I see. Anyway, go get some sleep for tomorrow's flight, and I will do my best for Anna to rest in peace," smiled Lucas.

"Thanks, I owe you one," Michael smiled back.

Michael watched Lucas walking back to his hotel. Before returning to his room, Michael visited the optical store nearby. "Hi, can you adjust these glasses?" said Michael as he handed Anna's glasses.

"Sure, do you know your measurements?"

"Actually, I just want you to make them normal. You know, replace the current one with normal lenses," explained Michael.

"Oh, I see. All right, but it will take a while, and we will close soon. So, can you come tomorrow to pick it up?"

"Um, sure. Then I'll come first thing tomorrow," Michael thanked the man, then returned to his suite.

After making sure everything was ready, Michael finally went to bed. He tried to sleep but then realized, without Anna's scent, he just couldn't sleep. Michael then rolled to Anna's side and he could at last close his restless eyes.

"That's better…"

REUNION

After a rough day, Michael could barely sleep that night. He sprung off bed twice, mumbling Anna's name. Michael eventually woke up around 5AM; his body was sweating like it never did before. "Finally, it's time to go," Michael wiped the sweat off his body in a haste, before heading for a cool shower. And after putting on some clothes, he had to make sure everything was packed, even Anna's stuff.

Michael went to the reception to check out, then walked to the optics store to pick his new glasses. "Oh, you're early. I just opened the store."

"Sorry, I'm in a rush," explained Michael.

"There you go," the man handed the glasses. Michael wore the glasses and remarked, "Yup, that'll do!" He then walked to the metro station, dragging two suitcases behind him.

"One way to Dubai Airport."

"That'll be twenty two Dirhams." Michael paid the woman, then headed to the platform. There, he waited for the first train to arrive.

Upon arriving at the airport, Michael checked in his

luggage, and went to the nearest café. He resumed reading Anna's diary. Despite feeling guilty for reading it, Michael couldn't help himself; for he wanted to understand Anna—the soft and emotional side of her.

Shortly afterwards, the flight was open for boarding. Michael walked to his seat in the very last row. He made sure that no one would book the seat next to him. After getting comfortable, Michael removed his newly acquired glasses and tried to shut both eyes to sleep

"Sir, would you like to eat something?" asked the flight attendant

Michael wiped his eyes then said, "Um, sure…"

"Would you like chicken or fish?"

"Hmm… Chicken please," answered Michael.

After eating, Michael checked the remaining time, "I have five more hours…"

"Back to sleep," Michael thought, as he drifted into the deeming world; where only there he would be able to call out for Anna and get a response.

"GOOD MORNING LADIES AND GENTLEMEN, as we are getting ready to—"

Michael quickly packed the blanket under his seat; he then returned his seat to the default position. The landing took thirty minutes or so, and the plane finally reached the gate. "Here we go…" muttered Michael.

Michael didn't tell Richard about Anna's death; and Richard was supposed to meet her outside, where Michael will be in a few minutes. Michael headed for the luggage belt;

he had to wait fifteen minutes for his luggage. Michael then strolled carefully towards the arrivals hall; where he found Richard standing near the exit.

Richard saw Michael approaching him, "Michael? What are you doing here? And are those Anna's glasses?"

"Mr. Richard, I want you to calm down a bit. Let's first exit the terminal." Michael then handed Anna's suitcases to Richard.

"I want an explanation immediately," demanded Richard, and Michael nodded accordingly.

"Anna won't come, she went to a better place…" Richard's face quickly turned pale, he grabbed Michael by his shoulders, "What do you mean? Don't play games with me! Where is my daughter?" Michael waited for Richard to release all his anger and regret. And after Richard let go, Michael began to explain, all the way from the beginning…

"Poor Anna…" Richard started to tear.

"Is he crying? What have I done! I thought he didn't care about her…" Michael thought. He then attempted to process what was going on before his very eyes. "Then… then have I prevented Anna from returning to her father? Her *pure* father…"

"Mr. Richard, throw your anger at me," demanded Michael, with tears on his cheeks.

"What are you saying?"

"I tried to stop Anna from returning, just because I suspected you. I thought you wanted to use her—just like my father."

"Is that so?" Richard hugged Michael.

"What's going on? I told him the truth and yet he… hugged me?" thought Michael.

"I'm sorry for encouraging Anna to escape. Just thought her parents were as bad as mine."

"It's all right, we kind of pushed her ourselves; me and Rita. What's with Anna's glasses?"

"Oh, they remind me of her. Sorry for being weird, but I feel as if Anna is seeing the world through my eyes." Richard smiled, "Is that so?"

"I bet you are hungry. Why don't you come to my place for lunch?"

"Sorry, I gotta search for a hotel. I'll stay here till after the funeral, then I'll head back to Dubai."

"Why don't you stay with me? Now that Rita and Anna are not here, the house feels larger than usual," explained Richard.

"After all that I did, I don't think I want to bother you anymore."

"It's all right don't take the whole blame," Richard took Anna's luggage then walked ahead of Michael to the car.

Michael ended up going along with him. After arriving, Michael found George waiting outside. "Michael? Wait, where is Anna?" he asked.

"It's a long story, George. Help Michael with the luggage," ordered Richard. George took the luggage and placed them in the guest room where Michael would stay. Michael then explained to George what had happened. While George didn't seem 'pleased'; yet, he didn't seem to be "mad" at Michael.

"It's all part of fate," noted George.

"I guess you're right..."

Both Michael and Richard ate lunch together. As he was lifting his fork, Richard remembered what happened three weeks ago, "When was the last time you called your parents?" he asked.

"I can't remember. But it was long ago. A month or so," answered Michael.

"So, you haven't heard?"

"Heard about what?" asked Michael, he then saw Richard's expression changing.

"Your father, Larry, went on a trip with Lisa. Mid-way, he lost control of the steering wheel, and the car fell off a cliff," Richard waited for Michael to show a response; alas Michael didn't.

"Lisa was lucky enough to survive, but she had lost her sight. And although she had survived, Larry didn't…" Richard stopped talking, having reached his last syllable.

Michael's first words were, "Oh… Is that so?" for the second time in his life, Michael did not know how to react.

"I'm sorry, I know it's hard for you to deal with this," apologized Richard. Michael didn't respond back; what could he possibly say?

"Larry died… My father died…" muttered Michael as reality slowly slammed his final wall of defense. He stood up and walked back to the guest room.

"You didn't finish your food, are you, all right?"

"Yeah, I'm just tired from the flight." Michael locked the door and stood in front of the mirror.

"Am I crying?" he noticed something on his face. Michael then proceeded to wipe the tears with his shirt, before covering himself with the blanket. He sobbed for a while before giving up to sleep.

MICHAEL'S PHONE WAS RINGING, "Now what," sighed he with a sleepy voice, tapping on the 'Answer' button, "Hello?"

"Michael, it's me, Lucas."

"Oh, hey Lucas. Any developments?"

"I just submitted her papers to the embassy. They told me it'll take three to four days before she arrives to LA. Also, I will have to return soon, since I didn't apply for any universities yet," explained Lucas.

"I see… Thanks for your efforts. I'll be waiting for you."

After hanging the call, Michael checked his phone's clock, "nine thirty, huh…" Michael was experiencing a severe case of jet lag. He had no idea what to do now, or for the remaining of the night for that matter. Michael was tired, but not sleepy.

"Richard, do you have a balcony or something like that?" asked Michael.

"Not exactly a balcony, but a place where I used to talk with Anna, will it do?"

"Yeah, can I go there?"

"Sure…" replied Richard.

Michael walked to where Richard and Anna used to hang out. He sat down and gazed at the stars. "What a beautiful sky tonight…" Michael said to himself. And as he was stargazing, Larry's image popped in his head; only for him to shake his head so that the image would disappear. A few moments later, the same image popped once again. "Why won't you leave me alone!" Snapped Michael.

Shortly afterwards, another image appeared. Yet, this time it was his family. Larry, Lisa and little Isabella. "Fine, I give up," Michael muttered. He then returned to Richard, who was holding a photo of Anna in his study room.

"Um, Richard. Do you have a car I could use?"

"Where are you going at this time?"

"I need to visit someone."

"You can take George's. His room is near the kitchen."

"Alright, thanks." Michael rushed to George's room, "George, may I have the keys?"

"Going somewhere?" asked George; Michael nodded.

George handed over the keys; and Michael hopped into the car and started driving. Midway, he realized, "Where is he anyway? If I'm not mistaken, we have two cemeteries here."

"I guess I'll have to search both," he sighed.

Michael arrived at the first one. He ran past the tombstones, one after another. "This will take forever…"

He soon stopped to catch his breath; as he was starting to regret coming here, the image appeared again. "All right, all right!" Michael ran through the whole cemetery, neither one was Larry's. He then drove to the second cemetery which was a ten-minute ride.

Once again, Michael began to run around the tombstones. And after reaching the fifth row, Michael saw someone.

"Who comes to the cemetery this late?" he thought. Michael's curiosity led him directly to the man standing by the grave. "David?"

"Michael? Is that you?" said the lady sitting in the wheelchair.

Michael snapped, "Mom? What are you doing here?" Michael could only see David as Lisa was hidden in the darkness.

"Michael, you returned… but why?" asked David.

"Stuff happened, stuff that I couldn't handle alone," spoke Michael, then faced his blind mother.

"Michael, come here!" Lisa raised her hands midair to hug Michael. Michael had no choice but to approach her. "I missed you, I really did…" sobbed Lisa.

Michael realized those tears came from her heart; he tried to cry in solidarity, but no tears came out. Michael then stood right next to Larry's tombstone. He stared at it for minutes without moving a muscle. Tears were sliding down his cheeks, "Why am I crying for someone like him? What's wrong with me," he muttered.

Lisa heard him, "It's normal for a boy to cry at his father's grave."

Michael wiped his tears, "All right. I have to go."

"Wait! Why did you return? What happened there? And where is Anna?" Lisa started to question Michael.

Michael turned back to Lisa. "She died," he said softly.

"Oh, I'm sorry to hear that. So, what will you do now? How about you live with me back at our—"

"I'm sorry, mom. I took an oath not to return to that place. Not after what I've experienced there. Plus, university starts next week. I need to get ready."

"Is that so? Then good luck with your life."

Michael smiled at David and then walked back to George's car.

"ANNA WAS MY EX-GIRLFRIEND. She was always laughing and had a smile on her face. I miss you Anna…" spoke Lucas, before walking past Anna and patting her forehead. Lucas then returned to his seat, eyeing the attending guests. It was Michael's turn, and he was the target of hatred. Rumors spread that Michael was the cause of Anna's stroke—that he killed her with his own hands.

"Anna was a precious friend of mine; we shared similar

dreams. She was willing to risk everything for her freedom. Too bad she didn't live to see the results." Michael paused, "In those three months, Anna changed my view on this world, she melted the coldness of my heart," he continued, taking notice of Anna's cousins staring at him. It was as if they were saying 'Just shut up already!' Michael knew that Rita was the one behind those rumors. After all, she came all the way to the funeral and sat near Anna's cousins. Michael then, following Lucas' example, went to Anna's tomb, kissed her, before waddling back to his seat. The whole room gasped, but it wasn't enough to halt the funeral's rather tight schedule.

After Anna was buried, people scattered all over the place. They wanted to return to their daily lives; only three men and one woman remained. Richard, Michael, Lucas and Rita were all standing by Anna's tombstone. "I won't forgive you, Michael, you killed my daughter!" snapped Rita.

Michael turned his head to face Rita, "We both know I—"

"Don't be silly, Rita! You were the one who encouraged her to escape!" interrupted Richard.

Rita shifted her eyes to Lucas; but Lucas didn't say anything. In fact, he didn't even care to look at her. His eyes were staring at Anna's tombstone. Rita thus walked away, and so did Richard shortly afterwards.

"You guys are coming?" he inquired.

"Lucas, go with Richard, I'll return later." Lucas nodded, and both returned.

Michael was once again alone with Anna. "You know Anna, I misjudged your father. I'm sorry about what I said about him. He truly wanted to be by your side." Michael then sat on the grass near Anna's tombstone. He grabbed her diary out of his pocket and started reading. Michael believed that this might be the last time he could talk to Anna. After all, his flight departs tonight.

"It's getting late, Anna, I have to go now. I will return to Dubai to continue my path. I won't forget you—ever!" promised Michael, before taking a leave to Richard's mansion. After packing his stuff, Michael went to George who was waiting for him near the entrance.

"All right let's go," ordered Michael.

George dropped Michael at the airport and then returned home. In his way, George passed by the cemetery to visit Anna and pay respect to the girl he has raised and saw grow all throughout her short-lived life...

I'm on my way to Dubai. Thankfully, no one's sitting next to me; the whole row was mine! Alas, I still don't feel satisfied. I feel that these past few months were strange—bizarre…

It all started with me deciding to escape; but now, it got out of hand. Anna, Taylor, Lucas; I had no idea that my foolishness would affect them all. Oh yeah, speaking of Taylor, did she marry the guy she wanted? Never mind that…

For as long as I could remember, I believed my life was mine to shape. No one had the right to change the road I was walking on. But eventually, I realized that I was a puppet in the hand of my parents this whole time. It just doesn't seem right; being controlled by someone else. But I think I'm slowly starting to understand the idea behind it. In the past, I was a puppet with no 'free-will'; therefore, I didn't have to worry about my actions' consequences. And because I was just acting according to how my puppeteers moved my strings, I couldn't be blamed. It appears that I wasn't ready to cut myself loose out of my puppet's strings; I didn't prepare myself enough. I was seeking freedom while not understanding its true meaning. Being free means that you are the master of yourself. Any word you say will have its effect and eventually, you will be accountable for it.

It started with my desire to get more; ended with me losing everything. I remember when my parents told me that what they were doing was for my own good. The way I see it, I killed Anna, and ruined Richard's marriage. All because of my so-called 'desire'. I'm not even sure whether it was worth the price I had to pay.

AFTER TEN HOURS OR SO, we landed at Dubai International Airport. I picked my luggage then hopped on the metro. I'm not sure where to stay now. Thanks to Larry's inherited money, I now have more, at least in theory. The man did one last service for his otherwise discarded son. For now, I think I'll settle in that same hotel. The service was good; plus, it's not that far from campus.

I checked into my hotel and went to my new room. There, I felt a strange desire to sleep, probably from the jet lag. Alas, I took a long breath then let it out at once; my guilt started to fade. I started to feel better about myself.

"I AM FREE!" I yelled from the top of my lungs; it's sure good to be guilt-free—or so I've been preaching of in disbelief...

ALSO BY IVORY RAVEN

A Desire to be Alive

Claire; Primed for Flesh

Michael; Inferior Past

Trevor; Hoaxed Affection

Scarlett; Fleshing Bright

Claire; Primed for Deception

THE JOURNEY CONTINUES...

Founded in 2021, **LJ Marshall's Publishing House** is an independent literary imprint of **Aoshiki Press** dedicated to the enduring power of the written word. We believe that thoughtfully composed stories possess the ability to stir the mind, challenge conventions, and echo long after the final page.

Our catalog focuses on works that explore the delicate boundary between fiction and the human psyche; stories that unsettle, inspire, and remain with the reader well beyond the moment they are finished.

📚 LOOKING FOR YOUR NEXT READ?

Discover more titles from our growing catalog, including poetry, mystery, and literary fiction.

Browse Our Book Collection!

www.ingramcontent.com/pod-product-compliance
Lightning Source LLC
Chambersburg PA
CBHW030143010826

48973CB00002B/698